A VERY MERRY SUPERHERO WEDDING

AN ADVENTURES OF LEWIS AND CLARKE NOVELLA

Kitty Bucholtz

For Linda,
Lots of wedding and
Christmas fun for you?
Love,
Kitty ☺

Daydreamer

Entertainment

A Very Merry Superhero Wedding

Published by Daydreamer Entertainment, 3520 Overland Avenue, #A-121, Los Angeles, CA 90034

Copyright © 2014 Kathleen Bucholtz

ISBN-13: 978-1-937719-11-1
ISBN-10: 1-937719-11-1

ISBN: 978-1-937719-10-4 (ebook)

Library of Congress Control Number: 2014922639

Cover design by John Bucholtz

Cover graphic of wedding invitation © Depositphotos.com/Ivan Baranov
Cover graphic of red bow © Depositphotos.com/Jinru Huang
Cover graphic of snowflakes © Depositphotos.com/Evgeny Illarionov

Edited by Marcy Weydemuller

Printed in the United States of America
Set in Adobe Garamond Pro

For Debra Holland and Brenna Aubrey,

and all my writing friends —

Thanks for helping me believe I could do it!

More Books by Kitty Bucholtz

Little Miss Lovesick

Adventures of Lewis and Clarke series:
"Superhero in Disguise"
A Very Merry Superhero Wedding
Unexpected Superhero

Short Stories in Anthologies:
Romancing the Pages ("Hero in Disguise")
Moonlit Encounters ("Rescue at Loon Lake")

CHAPTER 1

TWO things always surprised Joe Clarke in December: the weather, and the people of Double Bay.

Some years the snow would start falling by Halloween. Thanksgiving would be a day to have a plan B in case you couldn't make it to Grandma's house due to blowing and drifting snow. And Christmas would be both beautiful and frustrating with every outing marred by icy roads and fresh piles of snow to clear off the car.

Other years, like this year, there were a few snow showers, but hardly any of the snow stuck to the ground. The ski slopes were covered with machine-made snow. Shopping and traveling were a breeze.

And tracking potential home invaders proved more difficult.

Ah, yes, the wonderful citizens of Double Bay constantly surprised him. The young man he tracked now — that is, that his alter ego Superhero X tracked — really put the "dumb" in dumbed down. Not only was he peeking in windows in the fading light of the afternoon rather than waiting for the full dark that would fall over the city by dinnertime, but he wasn't paying attention to the security signs.

This particular yard sported a bold red and white sign near the front door — MGV Security. The sign wasn't hidden by snow either. What, did the guy think it was a Christmas decoration? Superhero X shook his head and waited. When the young man took out a pocket knife and pried the screen off one of the windows,

Superhero X moved closer and cleared his throat.

The man jumped and dropped his knife. His eyes widened as he looked up — way up — into the superhero's face. "Oh! I-I-I was just...I mean, I...I live here..."

X raised his eyebrows skeptically. "What's your address?"

"It's, uh, let me think, I just moved here and..." The man looked around the yard and at the other houses nearby, searching for a helpful clue.

Taking a long black zip tie from a pocket of his super suit, X gestured. "Hands."

The man sighed heavily and sagged against the siding. "You're not going to call the cops, are you?" He held out his hands. "I didn't take anything."

X tied the man's hands, then pressed a button on the wrist of his suit. "Superhero X to dispatch," he said. He gave the address, dispatch assured him that a police car would be there soon, then he marched the would-be Christmas thief to the sidewalk.

Pressing another button, he winced at the time. He'd have to hurry home to change after the police picked up the wannabe burglar. His fiancée, Tori Lewis, would be waiting for him — that is, for *Joe* — to pick her up from her last day at work. He didn't live far from here since this was his regular patrol neighborhood, but he still wanted to hurry.

Superhero X kept his facial expression impassive, but on the inside he could feel a grin. In five days, on Christmas Eve, he would finally marry the girl he rescued Halloween night. He could hardly wait.

Afraid a smile would break through and spoil his stern superhero expression, he brought his mind back around to work. He pressed a different button on his wrist and recorded a message with the time, the date, and the address of the house that had been broken into. Someone at MGV Security would get the information and call the homeowner to make a report.

"Someone" who was not Joe Clarke. MGV Security was a real security firm, but it was also Joe's cover job. A cover job from which

he was technically on vacation for the next two weeks. Owned and operated by Joe's friend and fellow superhero Mickey Valient, a.k.a. Tick Tock, MGV provided professional security services to all of its clients, but there were also more...*discreet*...services they provided the city.

A snowball whizzed overhead.

Superhero X turned to look down the sidewalk. Two boys around eight or ten years old stood frozen in their snow suits, mouths gaping. They'd collected what little snow was on their lawn and made a half dozen little snowballs, piled at their feet. X smiled and gave them a little salute. They whooped and jumped up and down. X grinned. He loved his job.

A Double Bay police car pulled up to the curb. Time to finish up work for the day and hightail it over to get his girl.

TORI Lewis felt butterflies square-dancing in her stomach. In a few minutes, she'd be off work to finish planning her wedding — and then she'd be away on her *honeymoon*. It almost didn't seem real.

For the last ten years or so, she had lived a quiet, semi-solitary life. Her mother Dixie and older sister Lexie were living proof that women in her family didn't make good choices when it came to men. Dixie's marriage to Tori's biological father had ended so badly that Dixie was still angry about it nearly twenty-five years later, even though her second marriage to Danny Lewis was filled with love and respect. Lexie had finally turned her life around a few years ago and found a "good" man to share it with. Then he broke it off and left when he found out she was pregnant. With those examples always on her mind, Tori had been afraid to chance the heartbreak and disaster she was sure would accompany a profession of love.

Until now.

There was something about Joe Clarke that called to a place

deep within. It was like he'd opened a tiny door inside her, and Tori was finding all kinds of treasures — a joyful hope, love without worry, a peaceful sense of relief that she could let down her guard and relax and be herself.

With Joe, she felt safe in a way she never had before. Since Danny became her dad, he'd provided a sense of security when the world tumbled crazily around her, but then Joe came along and Tori felt like everything was finally going to be all right.

No, not just all right. *Beautiful.* Her life felt beautiful all of a sudden.

She shook her head a little as she filed the last of the papers on her desk. She was being silly, all head-in-the-clouds like a Disney princess. That's apparently what love did to people.

It wasn't the drugs. A niggling doubt squirmed in her head, trying to get her attention and ruin her day. No, it wasn't only that she wasn't taking her medications anymore. She'd started Operation Freedom in September. She'd been working toward finding her real self when she met Joe just after Halloween. He seemed so strong and sure of himself, it gave her strength to push forward and make new choices.

And when he proposed on Thanksgiving Day, Tori knew the time had come for Operation Freedom's grand finale. No more Dr. Huntington and his drugs. No more kowtowing to her mother.

Yes, she'd been feeling better since she stopped taking the pills, but that couldn't account for how she felt about Joe. From the moment they met, they'd had a connection that was…well, it defied explanation. They both felt like they really *knew* each other. In sync, on the same wavelength, whatever you wanted to call it. And it seemed to grow stronger every day.

Tori let her worries fade as she shut down her computer. It was almost five o'clock. Joe would be here any minute. They had one more quiet evening together before the final rush toward Christmas Eve and their wedding. Her stomach felt the butterfly gymnastics again and she let out a soft giggle.

This was real. She and Joe loved each other with an urgency

and earnestness that made people fear they were merely infatuated with each other. But she knew — they both knew — it would last. They saw the world in similar ways. They believed in the same things. They'd prayed, together and individually, about the decision to get married. Waiting would only prove to others that they were ready. And they had nothing to prove.

"Oh, Tori," one of her co-workers singsonged nearby, "Someone's here to see you."

Tori's gaze flew to the doorway. There he stood. She sucked in a breath. His wavy brown hair was mussed, giving him a little boy look. So adorable. A knit cap stuck out of the pocket of his down-filled coat, and his scarf hung a foot longer on one side. Every time she saw him, he looked taller and more muscular than before. Every time she saw him, his smile made all of her nerve endings fire. Every time she saw him, she stopped breathing for a moment.

He grinned his lop-sided grin and chuckled. He always laughed when he saw her looking at him this way. Tori giggled and sighed. She knew he loved it, though. He'd told her no one had ever looked at him like she did.

Joe walked toward her and Tori felt a kind of tunnel vision come over her whole body. Every cell focused on him. And then he kissed her, and every cell burst out with a shout of joy.

Interrupted by the sound of laughter and clapping.

"Hello, beautiful," Joe whispered in her ear before he pulled away.

Tori felt her blood make a mad dash for her face. She'd never been so public in her displays of affection before Joe walked into her life. She'd been taking down Halloween decorations outside when he wandered by on a Sunday afternoon. They'd started talking and laughing and then they went for a walk together. Before she knew it, they were sharing a pizza. Then meeting again the next night, and the next.

And now here he was, staring down at her like he'd found a treasure he couldn't believe was his to keep. Tori realized she was grinning up at him only when more laughter and ribbing caught

her attention.

She stepped back and said, "Let me get my stuff and I'll be ready."

"Not so fast, lovebirds," called her boss, Faith Borden. "We need to send you off in style."

Faith pulled out a foil-covered tray and another co-worker cleared a space on a worktable. As Faith pulled off the foil, all the ladies broke into the "Happy Birthday" tune but with the words "Happy Wedding to You." On the tray were homemade Christmas cookies, each with a letter in icing spelling out "Congratulations Tori & Joe!" M&M'S candies, Tori's favorite stress reliever, decorated the tops.

Tori laughed and squeezed Joe's hand before she reached over to hug Faith and the others.

"Thank you, Faith," she said as she squeezed the woman who'd become a new friend. "This is wonderful."

"Good heavens, lady," Faith said in an undertone, "When you said he was gorgeous, I thought you were using hyperbole like every other bride. He's stunning!" She giggled.

Several similar comments followed, all in whispers hidden by the hugs. One woman offered to babysit any time Tori was out of town. Tori laughed and shook her head.

She looked over her shoulder at Joe talking to Faith. It was fun to be the envy of all the women in the room, but she didn't care much what other people thought. She knew Joe was a good man, decent and kind and hard-working and funny. He'd made her laugh more in the last seven weeks than she could remember laughing in the last couple years.

And he made her feel safe. And strong. Kind of like the Zorro character who'd helped her on Halloween after she'd been mugged. Zorro had joked about being a superhero and Tori had laughed and said, there's no such thing as superheroes, it's an anti-crime publicity stunt by the city. He'd argued with her, presumably because he was staying in character as a defender of the defenseless, and Tori had argued back. The spark she'd felt that night seemed to

lose some of its fire after that.

Then she'd met Joe two days later. At first, she thought maybe he was Zorro. But when she asked him, he laughed and said he was just an ordinary, everyday, average Joe. She'd thought that was funny. The more she got to know Joe, the less she thought about Zorro. The spark that night was nothing compared to the blazing fire that sprang up between her and Joe.

Studying him now, she knew nothing would ever put out that fire. Not the Lewis women's family curse. Not other people. Not time and old age. In five days, Joe's dad, Pastor Owen Clarke, would say the words, "What God has joined together, let no man separate." And that would be that.

For now, she needed to stop worrying that something would happen between today and Wednesday.

Joe caught her eye and nodded. She nodded back. Time to go. Tonight was the last night they would have alone together before they got married. Between the wedding and Christmas, it had been a busy month, and it would only get busier.

They said their goodbyes, Joe quickly accepted the rest of the cookies, and they made their way out to Joe's truck.

"They seem nice," Joe said. "Too bad you won't be working there again after the honeymoon."

"Yeah," Tori agreed, "I'd love to work for Faith. I hope her business grows enough that she can bring on permanent employees soon. Maybe I'll still be temping and she'll call me."

Tori smiled as Joe opened the truck door for her and handed her in. Such a gentleman.

"Are you sure you don't mind me temping for a while?" she asked when he climbed in the driver side. "I know I should probably get a real job, but I haven't found anything that makes me say, *this* is what I've been waiting my whole life to do. You know? I'm good with people. I'm a fast learner with tech stuff. But I haven't found a good mix yet. Maybe I should get a job at the Apple store," she joked.

Joe squeezed her hand as he pulled onto the street. "We'll

manage," he said, "whatever you decide to do."

Tori smiled at Joe's profile. Good man, through and through. She sighed. She was so lucky. So *blessed.*

Joe took her left hand and kissed her ring finger near her engagement ring. He held her hand while he made a turn, then he said with a grin, "You're staring."

Tori giggled. "Where are we going? This isn't the way home." They only lived a few blocks away from each other, so they obviously weren't going to either place right now.

Tomorrow, Joe's friends were going to move her belongings into Joe's house, and she'd stay with Lexie starting tomorrow night. The whole "moving into his house" concept still seemed surreal. She wondered how long it would take before she'd be comfortable saying "our" house.

"It's our last night alone for a few days, so I thought we should enjoy it."

"Um, you remember we have stuff we have to do tonight, right?"

"We still have to eat." He nibbled on one of her fingers until she giggled.

"Yes, yes, all right." Tori pulled at her hand. "Focus on your driving, mister."

Joe drove another ten minutes and pulled into the parking lot of a steakhouse Tori knew he loved. Actually, she wasn't sure if a steakhouse existed that he wouldn't love. Barely half-full at this hour, the restaurant provided quick service and hot, delicious food.

When Joe was nearly done with his steak, he cut another bite and paused. "You know I couldn't love you any less than I do right now. You know that, right?"

Tori put down her fork and lay her hand on his. "I feel the same way. It's crazy how much I love you," she said, feeling her throat tighten. "I can't imagine my life without you now."

Joe appeared to consider her words.

"Are you worried…" Tori felt a spike of anxiety lance her heart. "Do you think we shouldn't…"

It took a moment for Joe to follow her unspoken question. "No!" His startled expression underscored the truth of his denial, and Tori relaxed.

"You still want to, right?" he asked. He put down his fork and squeezed her hand.

"Oh, yes!" Tori chuckled in relief.

"Okay, good. No, I was just thinking...I wanted you to know that even though we haven't known each other very long, there's nothing you could do or say to make me love you less." He looked a little worried again. "Whatever we may learn about each other in the future."

Tori tried to figure out what was going on in his head. Was there something he wanted to tell her? Something he was afraid she'd find out? Something...oh no, something he'd found out about her?

She tried not to pull away. He loved her. She knew it. He'd just said it again, promised his feelings wouldn't change. "Has someone said something?" she asked, trying to focus on breathing evenly. "Told you something about me?"

"Oh, honey, no," Joe's expression changed again, back to his protective look. "There is nothing anyone could say that would change how I feel. I was just thinking that we haven't known each other very long, and...things are bound to come up that may surprise the other, and..." He shrugged. "I'm sure it will all be fine."

Ah, she got it now. He was afraid she wouldn't like something she might find out about him. She tried to lighten the mood. "You mean like if I found out you like country music?"

He made a face. "That is never going to happen. Metallica all the way, baby."

He'd said things before about not liking country. Tori pushed his buttons. "Or if you found out I like country music?"

"Don't even joke about that."

"Would you still love me if you found out I own some Garth Brooks CDs? It's great road trip music. You'll love it."

"That's not funny." Joe put one hand on his chest. "You're killing me."

She giggled. "Rascal Flats, too."

"Stop, just stop." Joe's comical expression morphed into laughter and he kissed her knuckles before letting go of her hand and picking up his fork.

"You're not an ax murderer," she said with a smile. "You haven't bilked thousands of people out of their retirement money, right? I can't imagine finding out anything bad about you."

She meant it, too. Joe was the epitome of Mr. Nice Guy.

"Maybe you'll learn more about my job, wish I were in a different line of work." His voice sounded casual.

Tori tried to soothe his concerns, whatever they were. "You work in security, keeping people safe," she said. "What's not to like about that? I'm proud of you, Joe. You walk your talk. I haven't met a lot of people who can do that. You're my hero." She gave him a flirtatious look.

Joe smiled and took her hand again, pulling it against his cheek. "Like a superhero?"

"No, a *real* hero. Not a Saturday morning cartoon. You really help people when they need it. That's a wonderful thing. I'd like to find a job like that."

Until recently, Tori had worked with the single-minded goal of making enough money to help take care of her nephew. Temp jobs with few benefits paid more than the full-time jobs she'd looked into, and she could take time off if Ben was sick. But now that Lexie was on her feet, Tori could start thinking about what she wanted to do with her life, not what she had to do.

"Come on," Joe said in a teasing voice, "wouldn't you like to meet a real superhero?"

"Like Batman?" Tori laughed. "If I ran into Batman in our neighborhood, he'd scare the crap out of me! Really, if you'd never seen any of the movies to know he was a good guy, you'd take one look at him and assume it was all over. Pearly gates, here I come."

Joe chuckled and shook his head. "Maybe. But I think if you

met a real superhero you'd know you were safe."

"*You're* the one who makes me feel safe," Tori said, pulling his hand to her lips and kissing it.

Joe looked like he was going to say something else, but the waiter interrupted to ask if they had room for dessert. Tori thought about the flourless chocolate cake she'd seen on the menu, but Joe told the waiter they'd pass.

"Eat too many cookies earlier?" she teased.

Joe raised his eyebrows a couple times. "You'll see. You want a to-go box?"

With the rest of her meal wrapped up, they put on their coats and gloves and hats and scarves. Even without much snow, the temperatures had dipped into the 20s every night not long after the sun went down.

Joe pulled her close as they walked to the truck. She loved his physical nature. His easy manner helped her to relax and allow herself to be a bit more demonstrative, in public and in private. She normally only let her guard down when she hung out with her siblings, especially with her little brother, Kevin. She'd spent so much energy over the years trying to please her mother, and staying away from men because they might ruin her life, she'd sort of lost herself. Hanging around Joe's excessively huggy family reminded her that she rather liked physical displays of affection.

She sighed happily.

Again Joe drove in a direction not toward home. He made a couple of turns into a residential neighborhood and hit the buttons to roll down the windows partway. What was he doing now?

Tori started to ask when she heard the Christmas music. She gasped in delight as Joe turned right and pulled into a long line of cars driving very slowly through the brightly lit street.

"Christmas lights?" She clapped her gloved hands. "That's one of my favorite parts of Christmas!"

CHAPTER 2

JOE grinned. The colored lights from the outside decorations danced over Tori's face. Driving around looking at Christmas lights was one of his favorite parts of Christmas, too. The more he and Tori got to know each other, the more they found in common.

Keeping his foot on the brake, Joe reached behind the seat and pulled several things to the front: a blanket, a thermos, and a plastic food container. He tucked the blanket around Tori's lap, letting his hands linger at her hips. Then he opened the thermos and poured the steaming beverage into the lid-cup.

"Hot chocolate?" Tori asked, reaching for the cup.

"Starbucks hot chocolate. Your favorite, right?"

Tori nodded and sipped and grinned. She was about to say something else when he opened the lid on the plastic container. Her eyes widened as she looked in.

"Triple chocolate cheesecake with a mint chocolate ganache topping. For my lady," Joe said, handing her a plastic fork with a flourish.

"Oh my gosh," Tori gushed. "Where in the world did you find something like this?" She scooped a bite onto her fork. "Oh, it's really cold! Mmm, but *awesome*."

Joe laughed. "I hope it didn't freeze in here while we were at dinner." He took a bite. Wow, delicious. "At least the mint flavor goes well with the cold."

The cars ahead of them moved slowly enough that Joe could drive with his knee while he shared the cheesecake with Tori. This

neighborhood had some of the best Christmas decorations in Double Bay. The house they were now passing had a Santa Claus scene with the sleigh and reindeer on the roof, Santa's rear end sticking out of the chimney, and an air-filled snowman directing a choir of singing children on the lawn.

The next house had a nativity scene with animatronic characters. Baby Jesus was waving his hands at Mary who was stroking his head while Joseph nodded. A young boy played a drum in time to "The Little Drummer Boy" music while an animatronic ox and lamb kept time with their nodding heads. The three wise men turned their heads to each other and then raised their arms to point at the star on the roof. The star was magnificent — at least five feet tall and glowing with a pulsing rainbow of pale colors.

"I'd say these people know about Bronner's in Frankenmuth." Tori laughed. "Have you been there?"

"Not yet. Been meaning to check it out sometime."

Tori gasped. "You haven't been to the world's largest Christmas store, and it's only a few hours away?"

Joe pretended his own shock with a gasp. "I can't believe I haven't taken time off work to go Christmas shopping." He opened his mouth wide and covered it with his fingertips.

Tori laughed and pushed at his shoulder. "If we had time, I'd take you there this year. Trust me, we *are* going next year."

"Fine." He really had been meaning to visit Bronner's. Just hadn't gotten around to it. It would be fun to let Tori show him around. She'd probably light up like a Christmas tree herself.

Sometimes she was very quiet, like she was trying to burrow into herself and hide. But when something caught her attention that she felt was important or that she had a strong opinion about, this vibrant woman appeared. That's what she was like when he met her on Halloween night. She was strong, tough, beautiful, and funny. He was smitten from the start.

If only she didn't have such strong feelings against superheroes. He wanted to find a way to change her mind tonight without spoiling the mood. How could he explain to her that she already

knew and loved a superhero? More than one, in fact, though he couldn't tell other peoples' secrets.

They drove past a couple more houses decorated with enough lights and decorations for most entire neighborhoods. "I don't even want to think about their electric bill," Joe said, shaking his head. "Just so you know, I'm not ever planning on doing this to our house. We'll just drive over here every year to look."

Tori chuckled and patted his hand. "We'll see."

The next house had a giant air-filled purple menorah in the center of the front lawn. A polar bear dressed in a sweater and knit cap played with a dreidel. Two more bears held a sign that read "Happy Hanukkah." More menorahs shone inside the windows. A wreath shaped like the Star of David decorated the front door.

Next came Joe's favorite house, and the reason for all of the slow-moving traffic. A light show flashed across the lawn, the garage door, and the roof with a loud upbeat mix of holiday songs playing along. The trees flashed on and off in time to the music, and different holiday greetings lit up on the roof and garage, flashing in a lively beat.

Tori laughed and watched the display for a couple minutes until they moved on. "I can't imagine how much work that must be, but I love it!"

She unfastened her seat belt and scooted into the middle of the truck's bench seat, snuggling up next to Joe. Putting one hand on his chin, she leaned over and kissed his cheek with a loud squeaking sound.

"You are the best, Joe Clarke. Thank you for all of this." She cuddled into his side as he put his arm around her shoulders. "This is the best last date I can imagine."

Joe chuckled and kissed the top of her head. "I'm glad you like it. But just because we're getting married doesn't mean we aren't going to do stuff like this anymore."

"Good to know," Tori said, eating the last bite of cheesecake. "If being married to you is at all like dating you, I'm going to be a very happy girl." She licked her fork. "Fat, but happy."

Joe laughed and kissed her. He wanted to kiss her more, but he couldn't while he was driving. Home. They should go home soon. While he was considering the relative merits of cutting short their night out, he noticed a furtive movement. A dark-clad figure stood in the shadows outside the house on the right. Joe braked as he'd done in front of other houses they'd admired.

No. Not now. What would he tell Tori? *I need to run out for a minute. Will you get behind the wheel and keep following this line of cars? I'll catch up to you as soon as I can.*

Right. And then when she pressed for an explanation? *I've been meaning to tell you, I'm a superhero. Kind of heir to the leadership, too. Even though you don't believe in superheroes, you're still going to marry me, right?*

Joe watched the punk, willing him not to do anything stupid. How did these guys think they could get away with breaking into houses with people around?

He squeezed Tori tighter. The bigger question might be, how did he think he could continue to keep his secret from her when they were married and living in the same house? He'd promised his parents he would tell Tori before the wedding. Surely she would believe he was one of the good guys, not a poser.

In Joe's superhero vernacular, those people were called Pretenders, and there were plenty of them. The colloquial "superhero" came from comic books, but people with powers had been called Paladins for thousands of years. Unless, of course, they used their powers for anything other than the protection of the human race.

While Joe didn't believe "villain" was a fair descriptor of many of those people, he was a product of his generation and tended to use the word too freely. Especially since he knew there were some truly nasty villains around, most notably The Nine. Thankfully, the one member of The Nine who had lived in Double Bay died a couple years back. The city became a much better place after his passing.

But this was the problem: as he tried to explain himself and his

abilities, Tori would likely have more and more questions, and he'd have to explain about the history of the Paladins, try to explain why so many people didn't know they existed, reassure her that their life would be pretty normal. She'd just have to accept that his job might be similar to that of a police officer or a government agent with him coming and going at all hours, in and out of danger, mostly working undercover.

And then she would ask about their children.

Joe shook his head slightly and kissed the top of her head. He couldn't tell her before the wedding. As determined as he'd been only a few months ago not to settle down too quickly, now all he wanted was a permanent tie to the woman in his arms. When they were married, he'd figure out a way to explain everything so that she would understand. He hoped, in fact, that she would embrace the challenges like his mother had, that she would partner with him as part of his support system. His mom could help show Tori what to do.

If he were so certain it would all work out — Joe could hear his dad's voice in his head — then he would tell her now. In fact, he would have told her before he proposed.

Another figure crept out of the darkness from behind the house Joe was watching. Great. What should he do? He couldn't run out as Joe and confront them. As he watched in indecision, the pair clasped hands and ran hunched over under the cover of trees, then walked sedately out to the sidewalk in front of the house next door. The first one opened the passenger door of a parked car, kissed the second one, and went around to the other side.

Teenagers. He should've known.

Joe decided to put his dilemma out of his head and enjoy his last date night with his bride-to-be. They spent another hour wandering around looking at Christmas lights. Then Tori made him laugh as she took a few selfies of them both and posted them to Facebook and Instagram. Eventually he turned his truck for home.

Their own neighborhood certainly looked different from the ones they'd been driving around. The asphalt on the street was

buckled and cracked. Half of the streetlights didn't work. There were Christmas lights along the roof eaves on many houses, but no expensive decorations on the lawns. Too easily stolen. The windows of many of the older houses were covered in heavy plastic to keep out the cold.

Joe had spent the money to put double-paned windows in his house before his first winter there, but he still needed to put better insulation in the walls. The city gave him the abandoned house two years ago on the condition that he live there undercover, patrolling the neighborhood as Superhero X. City officials wanted to test the theory that crime would drop in areas with more adjunct patrols. Of course, "undercover" meant not standing out, which meant not spending lots of money, so Joe still had a long list of home improvements he wanted to tackle.

Coming from a long line of superheroes who had saved and invested so that family members who wanted to work full-time had something to live on, Joe could afford a nicer house. But he and his team wanted the new Superhero Liaison Unit of the Double Bay Police Department to thrive and produce results so that the temporary unit would become permanent. They were willing to accept the city's terms, hoping that as they proved themselves, superheroes would be allowed to work more and more with the police. Including undercover work with the SLU.

He pulled into his driveway and shut off the truck. He'd turned on his porch light and Christmas lights before he left to pick up Tori so that they wouldn't return to a dark house. Looking at the place now, after touring those other areas, he decided he'd let Tori convince him to buy a few more decorations next year. They sat quietly for a moment, enjoying the lights of home.

"I like these icicle lights the best," she said. "It's funny how similar our tastes are. I don't think that's ever happened to me before." She chuckled. "Not that I've dated that much. Before I met you, I had grand plans for a full life as a single woman."

Joe grunted in agreement. "You and me both." Then he looked down at her. "Well, not the woman part."

Tori laughed up at him.

God, I love her so much. Please don't let me mess it up.

Joe leaned down slowly and placed a kiss on her lips, filled with all the promises he wanted to make. What if it wasn't enough to *want* to be a good husband, a good friend? What if he should have — but hadn't — learned an essential relational principle vital for building a great life?

He was beginning to see what his dad was getting at during the very little pre-marriage counseling Joe had agreed to. He and Tori had a lot to learn about being husband and wife, and not knowing each other very well would make the whole process more difficult.

But the loving part would be easy. He pulled back from the kiss, feeling himself get carried away. Five more days. It was only five more days, and Tori said she wanted to wait. Good thing it was already getting cold in the truck.

"We should probably go inside," he said. At the look on her face, he added, "To move things around and make room for your stuff."

"Soon," she said in answer to what they left unspoken.

Joe kissed her forehead and opened his door, welcoming the icy blast against his face. This was going to be the longest five days of his life.

TORI awoke slowly the next morning. She couldn't remember what she'd been dreaming about, but she remembered being happy. She stretched a little and then opened her eyes with a start. This wasn't her bed.

She looked around her former bedroom in Lexie's apartment. Oh, right. She grinned into her pillow. When she and Joe got to his house last night, they needed something to keep their minds off what they wanted to do to each other. Joe's newly-adopted cat, Snickers, a former stray he had been feeding for months, wandered

in from the living room demanding attention, food, and more attention.

Tori had teased Joe about the smell of cleaning products in his house, something she'd never noticed before. He stuttered for a moment before admitting he'd hired a cleaning service. He wanted the house to be as perfect as possible before she moved in. That had seemed a good segue into their task for the evening — moving furniture around and rearranging the closets to make space for Tori's belongings. Since she didn't have much — she'd only moved into her tiny studio apartment a few days before she met Joe — they were able to complete their task relatively quickly.

With nothing else that had to be done, she and Joe had cuddled in front of the fire to watch "A Charlie Brown Christmas" and "Dr. Seuss' How the Grinch Stole Christmas." But the stolen kisses during commercial breaks had morphed into stolen moments to watch favorite scenes from the shows in between kisses. And more than kisses.

Tori had called a halt to the progression, but Joe was already moving away before she finished her sentence so it must've been on his mind as well. When he took her home, the kissing goodbye part had become never-ending. Finally, she'd told Joe to give her a minute, she put together an overnight bag, and she'd directed him to take her to Lexie's. Nothing could happen there, not with her sister and nephew around. If it wasn't for the fact that their wedding was mere days away, Tori didn't think she or Joe would've been able to stop.

She grinned again. The anticipation was about killing her, but she knew it would be worth it. Only four more days and four more nights. She giggled. Yes, it was definitely a good thing she'd be sleeping at Lexie's for the next four nights. Then it would be her and Joe and a big bed at Disney's Grand Floridian Resort in Orlando.

Her musings were cut short by the sound of the door opening. A high-pitched shriek barely preceded the sound of tiny running feet. Tori looked over to see Lexie grinning at her three-year-old

son. Ben launched himself into Tori's waiting arms. She kissed him all over his face and head, the only parts besides his hands not covered in yellow fleece footy pajamas.

When he'd had enough, he sat up and began to tell her all about the last couple days of his life, everything she'd missed since she'd last seen him. Tori nodded and agreed that it all sounded very exciting. She only caught a few actual details — something about a dog and a soccer ball, and she was pretty sure he'd had pizza last night for dinner.

Lexie finally interrupted. "Let Aunt Tori get up, Ben. Come on, time for breakfast."

Ben jumped off the bed with a thud. "Pop Tarts, please?" he asked, running to his mother.

"Oh, so now you use your sentences." Lexie rolled her eyes at Tori. "Mom and Dad will be here at 9:30. Dad's taking Ben, and Mom's driving with us. Yay," she said with forced enthusiasm.

"We're going to have a fun day," Tori said. "What's not to love about trying on wedding dresses?"

Despite the fact that their mother Dixie loved them and did a lot for all three of them, she also could be a pain in the patootie. Nonetheless, Tori was determined not to fight with her mother this week, not a big fight anyway. Dixie had made it clear that she didn't approve of Tori's "hasty" wedding, but she was at least trying to come to terms with it.

They were almost ready when their parents knocked at 9:25. Lexie had Ben's shirt halfway on when he slipped away and ran to the front door as Tori opened it. Her dad Danny scooped up the toddler and motioned for his wife to precede him inside.

"There's my boy!" Danny said, jiggling a half-naked Ben in his arms. "Guess who gets to spend the day with Pop-pop?"

"Ben and Pop-pop," Ben squealed, clapping his hands.

"Give Grandma a kiss," Danny told him, handing the boy over.

Dixie cooed over him while she walked over to Lexie and the rest of Ben's clothes. "You need to be an octopus to dress them at

this age," she said to Lexie. "Can I help?"

Tori saw Lexie smile as she kissed Dixie hello. Whew. Looked like the day would go smoother than most.

Danny met her gaze and winked at her. "We're all going to play nice today," he whispered in her ear as he gave her a bear hug.

"Thanks, Dad," Tori whispered back. "I knew I could count on you."

"Now I'm not trying to start anything myself," he said quietly so that only Tori could hear him, "but just because you're doing the final fitting on your dress today doesn't mean you can't get off the train. I've got a shotgun in the car. I can whisk you away anytime you want."

Tori laughed. "You don't own a shotgun. And I'm not getting off the train, but thanks for asking."

"I rented one for your wedding. And you've got until the final 'I do' to change your mind." He held up his hand as Tori started to interrupt. "I'm not trying to stop the wedding, but these things can take on a life of their own and make you feel like you don't have any choices left. I just want to be sure you know that you *do* still have a choice. Humor me and say, 'Yes, Dad.'"

Tori grinned and hugged him again. "Yes, Daddy. Thank you. I'll let you know if you need the gun, okay?"

Danny kissed her forehead and shook his head. "Where's my little girl gone?"

"She hasn't gone anywhere," she said with an affectionate smile. "She's just adding someone new to the family."

"He seems nice enough, I guess. I'm not sure if he's good enough for you, but—"

"Okay, time to go," Tori interrupted, pushing away from her dad. She grabbed her purse, a duffle with the clothes she would change into for tonight's bachelorette party, and her wedding shoes to wear at the dress fitting. She pointed to a box of little gifts and prizes Lexie had wrapped for the bridal shower games, and Danny took it out to Lexie's car.

A fresh dusting of new snow covered the ground and cars. Just

enough to be beautiful and make it feel like Christmas. Perfect.

Dixie carried Ben outside, kissing his cheeks and making him giggle. "Honey, don't go to the mall with Ben, okay?" She handed Ben to her husband to buckle into the child seat.

"Why not?" Tori asked. "They have a S-A-N-T-A playground there that will keep him happy for an hour, at least."

"Haven't you heard about the ring of thieves targeting mall shoppers? It's just horrible. Breaking into cars, holding people up at gunpoint."

"I'm not sure there were any guns, honey," Danny said in a reassuring voice.

Dixie gave him "the look" and Tori watched her dad back down.

"But I promise, we won't go to the mall today," he said. He kissed her and turned her around toward Lexie's car. "Now go have fun. The men can take care of themselves."

Tori smiled at the exchange and opened the car door for her mom. Soon everyone was in the correct vehicle with the things they needed — Lexie almost forgot to give Danny the diaper bag — and off they went. Tori suddenly felt that surreal feeling come over her, like you wondered if you were dreaming or inside a movie or something. A movie dream where you got to be the bride.

Thank you, God, she said in her head. *Please let the rest of this week be filled with love and laughter and no arguing.*

An hour later, Tori stood on a dais looking at herself from half a dozen mirrored angles. Her breath caught in her throat. Today she saw herself in a way she never had before — beautiful. She caught her mother's eye. Dixie's chin trembled as she tried to restrain her tears. Then she gave it up.

"It's my blood right to cry when my babies get married," she said as she wiped at her cheeks. She sniffled and thanked the shop attendant when she handed Dixie a box of tissues.

Lexie walked out in her bridesmaid's dress. She stopped suddenly when she saw Tori. "Oh, Tori, you're stunning!"

Tori smiled at her sister and glanced back in the mirrors.

The white satin dress had clean, simple lines, cap sleeves, and a sweetheart neckline. Delicate lace fell from her waist partway down the skirt. The train trailed just a foot or two behind her.

She looked like a princess.

Joe was going to love this.

Tori's best friend, Hayley Addison, walked out in her bridesmaid's dress and stopped in her tracks. "Oh my gosh! Tori!"

Tori giggled. "This dress is a show-stopper, isn't it?"

"No." Hayley, generally full of something to say, paused as if looking for the right words. "*You* are the show-stopper."

Tori felt her eyes well up.

"She's right," Dixie said. And her face and tone conveyed that motherly love and pride that Tori so often longed for more of.

She stared at her mother in the mirror, smiling at her. This was one of those moments she needed to remember and cherish forever, especially when times were tough. "I love you, Mom." Tears rolled down her cheeks.

Suddenly all of the women jumped toward the dais.

"Don't let the tears fall on the dress!"

"The satin will stain!"

"Hand her the tissues!"

The box was shoved into her hands, but the woman doing the alterations had already pressed a linen handkerchief against Tori's cheeks. Tori took it and wiped her eyes, laughing at the attention. She glanced at the hanky. *Congratulations from everyone at Princess Bridal.*

"We had them made up for moments like this," the woman said.

Tori laughed. "Can my mom have one?" Dixie loved to collect little mementos from her children's milestones.

Dixie stepped onto the dais and took the hanky from Tori's hand, giving her the fresh one. She hugged her daughter tight. "I want to keep the one with my baby girl's happy tears on it, okay?"

"Oh, Mom," Tori said. Then they both laughed and cried at the same time, and everyone went crazy to protect her dress.

Hayley came to the rescue as she always had over the years. She called out orders and made jokes and helped push yet another emotional crisis behind them. Tori appreciated it. But this was one emotional crisis she would treasure.

CHAPTER 3

"EVEN though a certain Grandma is being silly," Danny said to the toddler in the back seat, "we'll keep our word and avoid the mall. However, we're still going Christmas shopping. I bet you've done about as much shopping as I have, right buddy?"

Ben stared at Danny in the mirror, then turned away to look out the window.

"Just as I thought," Danny said, hitting his turn signal. "It's only the twentieth. We have five whole days before Christmas. I bet we can get everything we need today. Men are good like that." He turned into the bank parking lot and pulled into a space on the side near the ATM. "You stay here, I'll be right back."

Even though he didn't worry about being robbed at the mall — he wasn't a small man and felt confident he could take care of himself — he was always extra careful with his grandson. He took his keys and locked the car. At the ATM, he turned to wave at Ben. No tantrums, good. That's one of the things he liked about his grandson.

Danny opened his wallet and pulled out his ATM card. Before he could slide it into the machine, he heard someone else walk up. He turned to see a young man in a dark coat, dark knit cap, and gloves walking toward him. It wasn't cold enough outside for anyone to need their collar pulled up around their face.

He smiled and nodded at the man, and turned back to his car. "Wrong card," he said.

From behind him, another voice said, "Why don't you try it

anyway?" Someone pushed him roughly toward the ATM.

Danny turned to look at the new guy and weighed his options. This fella looked like he was up for a fight. While Danny considered how to best land his punches, the new guy opened up a switchblade knife. The odds shifted further out of his favor.

Danny forced himself not to look toward Ben. They might get his money, but he wouldn't give them his keys, not even at knifepoint.

He decided to play the scared older guy. He let his hands shake and dropped his card. "You take it," he said, "I don't want any trouble."

He backed up a step toward the first man, purposely landing hard on the guy's instep. The man cursed and shoved him. Danny let himself be propelled farther away from the ATM. Now how could he reach for his keys and get into his car before they overpowered him?

The second man lunged for Danny and shoved him hard toward the cash machine. "Withdraw four hundred dollars. Now." He held the knife near Danny's face and pushed the card into the machine.

Unfortunately, this guy seemed to know exactly what he was doing. Fine, maybe they'd leave with the money, and he and Ben could go safely home. Where he'd pour himself a stiff drink perhaps.

Danny looked around for cameras, police cars, other people, any distraction. Seeing only the dark glass that likely covered the bank's hidden camera, he made a point of looking fully into the glass for a moment. If the worst happened, at least the police would be able to identify him.

"Enter your PIN."

Danny typed it in wrong, buying time. Surely the bank parking lot had some kind of security service doing rounds. He remembered to make his hands shake, which wasn't too hard. "You've got me all flustered."

"You don't look like the easily flustered type," the leader said harshly. "Do it right, or you'll have a scar to remember and I'll take

your car."

Danny's heart froze.

"Yeah, I saw the kid. Now enter your PIN!"

His hands shaking for real, Danny carefully entered the correct number. He pushed the button for Withdrawal and then the one for Checking Account. He was about to reassure the leader that he would withdraw the maximum amount when a third voice spoke up.

"Didn't your mother ever tell you not to play with knives?"

Danny looked up in surprise. A massive hulk of a man stood calmly to one side, his arms folded over his chest. He wore an outfit that could've come out of one of the *X-Men* movies. Something disguised his voice so that it had a metallic sound.

The man's expression flickered for a moment as he glanced at Danny, as if he were surprised. Then his focus returned to the man with the knife.

Danny heard the other robber stutter and turn to run. A cheerful man's voice said, "Not so fast." Danny turned to see another strangely costumed man stretch out his leg and trip the robber.

Danny blinked hard. What...?

The robber got up to run again, but the costumed man stretched out his arm — yes, he was seeing what he thought he was seeing — the man stretched his arm at least four feet and grabbed the robber's collar. Then he stretched his leg out — several feet longer than should've been possible — and tripped the fella again. All without moving from where he stood.

Like Danny, the knife-wielding robber just stood and stared.

The big man moved forward to grab the leader. The leader turned quickly, bringing the knife in low and fast.

"Watch it!" Danny called.

But the big man didn't move. The knife hit him squarely in the stomach...and didn't sink in. Did the man have Kevlar in his outfit?

Before Danny could understand what was happening, the two

costumed men had shoved the two robbers against a post, back-to-back, and zip-tied their hands together. The big guy took the switchblade knife and hit the button to send the knife back into the handle with a click. Then he grabbed both ends of the knife and twisted his hands down.

Danny gaped. The man had bent the knife at a thirty-degree angle. With his bare hands.

"Who *are* you?" Danny heard his voice crack.

"Stretch and Superhero X, at your service." The wiry man who could move in unnatural ways bowed and grinned. He extended his hand and Danny numbly reached forward to shake it. It felt like a normal hand.

"Show off," muttered the big guy. "Your card is still in the ATM, sir. Did they get anything from you? Hurt you in any way? The police will be here soon. You'll need to stay and make a report. You can wait in your car with the doors locked, if you like. We'll wait here until the officers arrive."

Danny nodded and hit the buttons on the machine to get his card back. When he turned, he saw the big man leaning over and looking in the window of his car. The man's fingers squeezed together twice, imitating Ben's childish wave from inside. Danny saw the man smile, and Ben shrieked with laughter, kicking his legs against his car seat and reaching toward the window.

The man stood up, saw Danny watching, and cleared his throat, wiping any expression from his face.

"I-I don't understand," he said to the big man. He turned to the other guy. "Who are you again?"

Both men's costumes covered a good deal of their faces. All he could see was a strong white chin on the big guy, and an angular black chin on the wiry fella. The man who called himself Stretch didn't disguise his voice. Maybe Danny could pick it out again later if he needed to. Despite the fact that he practiced real estate law and had never dealt with criminal cases, his attorney instincts were running high. But he had very little to go on if he ever wanted to describe these two to the authorities.

"We work with the police, sir," said the big one. He turned aside slightly and didn't meet Danny's intent gaze. "Ah, here they are now."

Did the man sound relieved? Why would that be? *How* did they work with the police? And where had they come from? Who were these men?

The lawyer-like questions ran through his mind, but inside Danny had known the truth minutes ago. Despite all Dixie's insistence over the years that there was no way, these men were… well, he didn't know another word.

Superheroes.

It was true.

He'd held onto disbelief all these years because it would upset his wife if he allowed himself to wonder aloud. If he didn't believe in superheroes — or super villains — then his daughters had never been in danger, would never be in that kind of danger.

But now…

Danny shook his head as he tried to focus on the policeman now standing in front of him. "What?"

The officer pointed to Danny's car. "Why don't you turn on the engine before your son gets too cold," he suggested. "I can question you over there."

Danny did as he was asked, turning the heat to high, and reaching into the back seat to reassure himself that Ben was fine. He turned back to the policeman and looked around for the… superheroes.

But they'd disappeared.

CHAPTER 4

WITH all of the dress alterations approved, the women piled into their cars and drove to the church. Tori used to think of it as Joe's church, or Pastor Owen's, but she had recently started attending with Joe, so she supposed it was her church now, too. Hannah, Joe's mom, had asked to host the bridal shower there since so many people were expected.

The "so many people" part kind of freaked Tori out, but she wasn't allowed much of a voice. Both mothers, her sister, and her best friend had worked together planning the party, and Tori had been told in no uncertain terms that the guest of honor didn't get a say. In fact, there would be even more people than might otherwise be expected due to family from both sides visiting from out of town for the holidays.

Tori led the way downstairs to the fellowship hall in the basement. When she came around the corner, her younger sister Sam yelled, "Surprise!" and flung her arms out to show Tori the decorated room. It looked amazing.

Pale green and white streamers dipped and curled from one end of the ceiling to the other. Twinkling white Christmas lights added a magical feel. Red silk roses decorated the tables in glass vases filled with green beads. The tables were covered with an alternating pattern of red and green Christmas tablecloths, and white tablecloths with silver doves and wedding bells.

An enormous amount of food covered several tables — pans over burning Sternos for hot dishes, bowls of salads and pastas, a

full table of desserts. Tori could see half a dozen women bustling about the church kitchen preparing more food.

"Wow," was all she could say.

"Do you like it?" Sam asked, giving her a hug.

"Sam headed the decorating committee," Lexie said, giving their little sister an affectionate squeeze.

"I love it," Tori said, still staring around the room. She looked closer at the nearest table — yes, little bowls of red and green M&M'S sat on each table. She grinned. Her sisters knew her well.

She noticed little Christmas trees on some of the tables, each topped with a pair of tiny white doves.

"The Christmas trees are from Hayley's nursery," Sam told her. "She decorated all of them herself."

"Hayley," Tori exclaimed, giving her best friend a hug, "they're beautiful."

"And they double as game prizes," Hayley said. "Lex thought people might like them."

"What I *said*," Lexie interrupted, "was that people would *love* them."

Tori let Sam take her coat while people pulled her farther into the room. There were dozens of people there, many of whom Tori was pretty sure she didn't know.

Hannah rushed over and hugged everyone, giving Tori a teary-eyed squeeze. "I can hardly believe you're going to be my new daughter in a few days." Then she hugged Dixie, took them both by the arm, and promised to introduce them to all of the women on Joe's side of the family. "Don't worry, there won't be a quiz."

A few of them, Tori had already met. Joe's twin sisters, Gwen and Daphne, and his youngest sister Melissa, who was a year younger than Sam, had been at Thanksgiving dinner and had gushed over Joe's unexpected proposal.

Then there were Joe's sisters-in-law, Brenda and Amy, and their young daughters, Katie and Ashley. There were several aunts and a boatload of cousins. Wow, and these were just the female relatives! How many people was Joe related to?

"These two darlings," Hannah hugged Katie and Ashley to her sides, "volunteered to play with the children in the Sunday School room after we eat. That way whatever happens in here, stays amongst us adults." Hannah winked at Tori.

Before Tori could decide if she should be worried about what exactly was going to happen, what could only be described as a small white whirlwind rushed over from the kitchen. An older woman, who could have been a stand-in for Olympia Dukakis, embraced Tori with exuberance. She stood back, hands gripping Tori's shoulders, and appraised her from head to toe.

"This must be my new granddaughter, Victoria!" the woman declared. She gave Tori another bear hug.

Tori tried to keep a friendly smile on her face, but she'd already been feeling a bit overwhelmed from the onslaught of familial attention. This new attack threatened to push her over the edge. In her own family, she was the quiet one. People were generally friendly, but mostly they thought she and Lexie were a bit odd, so they didn't engage them in long conversations.

Or long hugs. The white-haired woman appeared to be coming at her again.

"Millie, stop." Hannah laughed. "You're scaring the poor girl. Tori, Dixie, I'd like to introduce Millie Clarke, Owen's mom and Joe's grandmother. And the most fun mother-in-law in the world."

Millie grabbed Dixie for a quick hug, eliciting an "Oh! Hello!" from Dixie, then she turned back to Tori. "You can call me Nana," she said firmly. "All the grandkids do. I think it's destiny that Jonas is marrying a girl named for victory." She leaned in closer and continued in a conspiratorial stage whisper. "Since he's—"

"You're favorite," Hannah interrupted with a laugh. "Yes, yes, we know."

Millie glanced up at Hannah and Tori saw something pass between them. "Yes, my favorite." She turned back to Tori. "I know I shouldn't pick favorites, but..." She shrugged.

"Is everything ready?" Hannah asked.

The whirlwind rushed around the room, Lexie was given a

microphone and she and Hayley welcomed everyone, then people lined up to eat lunch before the games began.

Tori was pulled to the front of the line. She looked for someone safe to grab onto. Her friends Liz and Gabrielle stood nearby. "Liz! Gabe!" she gushed as she hugged them hello. "I'm so glad you came." In an undertone, she said, "Stand with me. I'm freaking out at all the attention."

They laughed and the three of them grabbed plates, oohing and ahhing over the delicious-smelling dishes.

Liz leaned close and said in a low, excited voice, "So tell us, what's the fuss with the rushed wedding? Are we planning a baby shower soon, too?" She giggled.

Gabe spoke up before Tori could reply. "I saw the pictures you posted on Facebook last night. Dang, girl, he's *hot*. No one would be blaming you for saying yes to that."

Tori felt herself blush. It was one thing to be teased by your friends, but another thing entirely when family might be listening. "No! I'm not — I haven't — we're getting married because we *want* to."

"Well, who wouldn't want to marry that hunk," Liz said, putting a couple of hot wings on her plate. "But you just met him, didn't you?"

"Oh!" exclaimed Gabe. "Unless you have been secretly dating him for months and didn't want anyone to know. That would be so romantic." She sighed theatrically.

Tori laughed, and moved to the desserts table, out of earshot of family. "No, no secrets." Well, not the kind they were talking about anyway. She hadn't told Joe about the shrink and the meds and the years of being thought of as a bit of a freak. But she had put all that behind her, so there was no reason to tell him. Not until they were old and gray and he was so far beyond in love with her that it wouldn't matter.

She took a big breath. She wanted to tell someone and have them understand. Her family wasn't really listening. "You know those stories about love at first sight?" She looked at both

of her romance-minded friends, willing them to believe her and understand and be happy for her. "It was kind of like that, but it took a few hours rather than a few moments." She giggled. "It was love at first date, I guess, since we eventually ate dinner together."

Gabe got a mushy look on her face. "Aww. That's so adorable."

"It is adorable," agreed Liz. She looked over her shoulder. "So why do I feel like it's a secret?"

"You know my family. They're very practical and…" She searched for a word. "Careful. Mom says if I'm so sure I'm in love with him, I'll still be in love with him next summer and I should get married then." She worked hard not to let any bitterness creep into her voice.

"Parents." Liz shook her head. "They seriously need to relax."

"And remember what it was like to be young and in love," Gabe added. "They must've been young and in love once."

The girls giggled together and started to sit down to eat. But Hayley came over and apologized and said the bride had to sit at the middle table where everyone could see her.

Tori looked out over the crowded room.

Hayley squeezed her shoulder and picked up her plate. "You'll be fine," she said, understanding. "I'm sitting on one side of you and Lexie will be on the other. Come on."

"This is why we're having a small wedding," she said. "So I don't have to stand up in front of crowds of people."

"Well, you still aren't," Gabe said, chuckling. "You'll be sitting. Not so bad. We'll cheer you on from here."

Tori smiled at her friends and let Hayley pull her away. She began to relax a little as everyone sat down to eat and talk amongst themselves. "You all really outdid yourselves," she said to her sisters, both mothers, and Hayley, all seated with her. "Thank you so much."

Sam giggled. "Just wait until the games begin." She had an impish look Tori hadn't seen in awhile. Sam's first semester at college had brought out old insecurities and anxiety. It was good to see her laughing.

The games were the fairly typical ones for bridal showers. Timed lists, word searches, purse raid. It was more fun than Tori thought it would be. And she was getting to know her in-laws-to-be as well as seeing her own cousins and aunts in a new light. Even the relatives she thought of as the conservative ones had relaxed in the spirit of the games.

When the purse raid game finished, Sam rose and set up an easel, then pulled a covered board from behind a table. Tori watched her suspiciously, a half smile on her face, because Sam kept glancing at her and giggling.

Lexie retrieved something from a bag next to her and stood up. "Okay, everyone, this next game is the most important one so it has the *biggest* prize." She held up a huge box of condoms for everyone to see. The crowd laughed.

Tori gasped and covered her mouth, choking on a laugh. She looked over at her mom and Hannah. Both women laughed easily, not looking embarrassed. If they weren't, she'd try not to be either.

"To play," Lexie continued, "we have this box of condoms, this blindfold—"

People laughed and hooted. A few whistles and boisterous yells pierced the air.

Tori shook her head and covered her eyes. Oh my gosh. She could feel her cheeks getting hotter.

"This box of colored pushpins," said Sam from in front of the easel, "and…" She pulled the cover off the board with a flourish.

A huge poster of The Avengers taped to foam core generated more laughter.

Tori noticed Joe's family laughing harder than anyone else. Maybe they'd played this game before.

Hayley elbowed Tori and nodded to the poster with a big grin. "You'll never win at this," she whispered. "You don't know what to do, right?"

Tori stuck her tongue out. Hayley laughed and hugged her shoulders.

"What you'll do," said Lexie to the room, "is open a condom,

unroll it," she did so as she walked over to where Sam stood, "put a push-pin in the top here, spin around three times, and pin it on the poster as close to the correct piece of anatomy as possible. Blind-folded."

"Oh. My. Gosh." Tori looked at Hayley and shook her head. "What were you two drinking?"

Hayley laughed, but before she could say anything, Dixie leaned over and patted Tori's hand.

"Don't worry, sweetheart, you'll get the hang of it after a while."

"Mom!" Tori gasped and laughed and covered her mouth. She was sure she'd never in her life heard her mother say something like that. It was both disturbing and hysterical.

"She's right, Tori," Hayley whispered in her ear. "Getting it on is the hard part. Getting it off is easy."

"Hayley Addison! I'm never going to be able to get that out of my head," Tori whispered back, wiping the tears from her eyes as she laughed.

"Okay, everybody," Lexie called to the room. "Come on up. The bride will go last. She'll have to beat all the other — um, *scores* — on the board."

The next few minutes were side-splitting fun. The condoms were attached to the most unusual places on The Avengers poster. Some people got so disoriented after being spun around three times that they walked off to the side of the poster, blindly flailing their arms around to the vast amusement of the onlookers. Lexie would give them a little nudge in the right direction, and the condom would land someplace ridiculous. One was currently hanging off the end of The Hulk's nose.

A little old woman stood next in line. She handed her cane to Lexie and snapped her fingers for a condom. Joe's relatives grinned and called out encouragement.

"That's Millie's mom, Esther," Hannah said to Tori and their table. "Owen's grandma, Joe's great-grandma."

At the easel, Lexie gently tied the blindfold over Grandma Esther's eyes but didn't spin her around. Grandma Esther took her

cane firmly in one hand, stood quietly for a moment, then shuffled up to the poster with her other arm outstretched. As soon as her hand hit the poster, she pushed the pin in.

Everyone laughed. The condom was pinned directly to the appropriate part of Thor.

"What? Didn't I do it right?" Grandma Esther asked, trying to get the blindfold off.

Lexie helped her, laughing. "No, you were great. Look, you've done the best so far!"

Grandma Esther moved forward to take a closer look. Then she turned to the room and said in a matter-of-fact voice, "Well, I do have the most experience."

The entire room exploded. All the women were holding their sides and wiping their eyes, they laughed so hard.

Tori couldn't talk, she could hardly breathe. But she wanted to say, this is the most fun party I've ever had!

"Tori! Get Tori!" someone called.

"It's the bride's turn!"

"Bring down the bride!"

Tori got up and stood next to Lexie and Sam. "I don't think I can follow that," she said to Joe's great-grandma. She leaned down and gave her a gentle hug and a kiss on the cheek.

"I can show you if you want," Grandma Esther said in a voice loud enough to carry.

Everyone laughed and Tori blushed some more. "No, thank you, I'll manage."

Lexie turned her to face the room, then tied the blindfold around her eyes. "Wait, you have to give me a condom first," she told her sister.

"Oh no," Lexie replied. "You need to learn to do this in the dark."

More laughter.

Tori opened the condom wrapper, but when she pulled the condom out, it slipped through her fingers onto the floor. Oh boy, was this an embarrassing game. She started to bend her knees, but

Lexie pulled her arm, giggling.

"Here, just take a new one."

This time, Tori was careful not to drop it. She laughed as people called out directions on how to unroll it. When she finally got it to its full length, she played along with the crowd, holding it up and asking, "Is it long enough now?"

"You'll find out in four days!" someone called out.

Tori felt Sam's hand on hers, and she put a pushpin in the top of the latex. Then she felt both sisters spinning her around. When they stopped, Tori put her arm out, but Lexie must've been gesturing to the crowd because everyone laughed again.

"Nope, not yet," Sam giggled.

Then they spun her around the other way. Tori nearly fell over, she was so dizzy. Her sisters let go of her and when she took a step forward, they took turns saying "warm" and "cold" and "warmer" until Tori could reach out and feel the poster.

She started to push the pin in, then moved her hand to another area. Someone called out "Ice cold!" and Tori moved her hand again. More people called out advice, some of it quite risqué, until Tori finally pushed the pin into the foam core.

By the time she was done, the room echoed with hilarity.

Tori pulled off her blindfold. Her condom was pinned to Captain America's shield. "Well, it's sort of close to the right part of Iron Man," she said with a grin.

"Close, but not close enough," Lexie said. "The winner of Pin the Condom on the Avengers Poster is Grandma Esther!"

Sam pulled out a big basket wrapped in cellophane. Tori saw it was filled with scented products from Bath & Body Works. Sam handed it to Tori, and Tori walked it over to Grandma Esther.

"Why, thank you, lovey," said her about-to-be-great-grandma. She reached up for Tori to hug her. "Don't worry," she whispered in Tori's ear, "his powers are nothing to be afraid of. You'll be fine."

Tori was so glad no one else heard that. How embarrassing! His "powers"? Was that how people used to talk about sex? She pulled away before Grandma Esther gave her a lecture on the birds

and the bees.

When she walked back to her sisters, face burning, she was so relieved to find the games were over. Hayley motioned her over to the gifts table. Okay, good, that would be easier on her nerves.

Lexie handed her presents, Hayley wrote down who they were from in a little white book, and Sam took all the ribbons, doing something with them out of Tori's view.

The gifts overwhelmed Tori with the generosity and creativity of the givers. There were kitchen items, including a Crock-Pot and matching cookbook, silver picture frames, baskets of soaps and bath salts and lotions, and pre-made "date night" packages with gift cards for restaurants and the local movie theater chain.

While Lexie took a moment to figure out which gift went with a card, Tori leaned over and whispered to her mother. "This is wonderful, but it seems like too much. I'm stunned and…" She shook her head a little.

Dixie hugged Tori's shoulders and kissed her cheek. "I know you don't like to be the center of attention, but this is your *one* day, sweetheart. Relax and enjoy it." She smiled warmly. "It's only going to happen one more time in your life, and then it won't be about you as much as it'll be about your unborn baby. Today, all these people are here to congratulate you and welcome you into their family. They need to believe you're enjoying this. It's your gift back to them."

Tori thought about the times she'd been on the other side of this table. She absolutely loved to watch people unwrap the presents she gave them. It was fun to see their faces light up, no matter whose gift they opened. She took a deep, calming breath.

Okay, God, help me to give them a gift, too.

Lexie figured which gift bag a card went with and handed both to Tori.

"This one is from Liz," Tori said and waved her fingers at her friend. She read the card, laughing at the message, then opened the gift bag. She pulled out a small box and opened it. It was a beautiful silver necklace with two hearts joined together.

"'First comes love'," she read aloud from the tag inside. "This is beautiful, Liz."

She pulled a large box wrapped in tissue paper out of the gift bag. "'Then comes marriage'," she read from another tag taped to the outside. She pulled off the tissue paper and sucked in her breath. The box was decoupaged in all kinds of pictures and little decorations.

There were pictures of Tori and Joe that she remembered posting on her Facebook page. Pictures from a bridal magazine, pictures from a home and garden magazine, and words like "love" and "forever." Four black picture corners in the center of the top of the box waited for a new photo.

Tori opened the box to find the inside decorated as beautifully as the outside. Lying on the bottom of the box was a picture of Liz and Tori in front of one of the big roller coasters at Cedar Point in Ohio. It was taken in junior high when the church youth group went down for a weekend. Liz had decorated the picture to make it look like a Polaroid. On the bottom, she'd written "Best day ever — until now."

Tori teared up. She couldn't read it aloud. "Tissues, please!" she barely got out.

Sam ran for tissues while Hayley leaned over Tori's shoulder and described the gift to the crowd. "Aww, that's so sweet, Liz."

Several people joined in with "Aww."

Tori held the picture to her heart and smiled at her friend. "I'm framing this," she told her.

Liz picked up her napkin and dabbed at her eyes. She waved her hand at the bag. "Keep going. There's one more."

Tori reached inside and drew out another tissue-wrapped bundle with one more note. "'Then comes a baby in a baby carriage!'" Tori rolled her eyes and grinned. So much for trying to convince Liz there was no baby coming soon. She unrolled a piece of cloth to find a cute baby rattle. Unfolding the cloth, she found a hand painted baby bib. Amid the colorful pictures it read, "I love Aunt Liz."

Tori laughed and held it up for people to see. "Thank you, but don't be offended if I don't use it for a couple of years," she said to Liz.

Her friend shrugged. "The best laid plans…"

Sam took Liz's gifts and carefully fit everything back in the bag. Then Lexie handed her more presents. Tori remembered what her mom said and made sure everyone could tell how much she loved everything.

There were handmade Christmas ornaments with their names and wedding date, a set of four hand-tatted lace doilies shaped like snowflakes, a satin bathrobe that was definitely not for staying warm, and so much more.

Or less, depending on how you looked at it. Hayley gave her a barely-there teddy from Victoria's Secret. "Really, Hayley," Tori said loudly so everyone could hear. "You couldn't give me something like this in private?" Then she leaned over and hugged her. "It's beautiful, thank you."

"Just don't tell me anything more than 'he liked it,' okay?" Hayley laughed.

After Tori opened the last gift, Sam presented her with her bridal shower ribbon bouquet. Tori didn't know how she'd done it, but Sam had twisted some of the ribbons into flowers, braided others to make an edging, and left trailing tendrils to hang from Tori's hands when she held the bouquet. She'd also braided the silver and white ribbons together to create a headpiece that looked like something out of a Disney movie.

"Sam," Tori breathed as Sam arranged the ribbons on her hair. "This is beautiful." She hugged her little sister tight. Since they hadn't lived in the same house for several years, Tori hadn't realized how much she didn't know about Sam, like how artistic she was. "Wow."

All the ladies ooh'd and ahh'd and suddenly everyone had a phone or a camera in hand, taking pictures. Tori smiled and grinned and hugged and laughed and smiled some more. By the time the last of the guests had left, her cheeks ached. But her heart

was overflowing.

"Lex, Hayley, Sam, that was wonderful. Really beautiful." She hugged them each in turn. "Thank you so much. That was the loveliest shower I could have imagined."

She turned to Joe's mom. "Hannah, thank you so much for this. I hope your family thinks I'm..." She fluttered her hand, trying to think of a word better than "okay."

Hannah hugged her tight. "They think you're wonderful," she said. "You and your whole family."

Tori smiled and felt her usual quieter self return. She ducked her head to hide the blush she feared was blooming. "Oh...well, good. Um, do you need help cleaning up?"

"You girls go on, I've got it covered." Hannah pointed behind Tori to four women coming down the stairs. "The troops have arrived." At Tori's questioning glance, she clarified, "My Bible study offered to do the cleanup today."

The ladies waved and called out greetings to each other. Tori recognized one woman, but didn't know her name. These strangers had come to help make her day perfect. Wow.

Tori turned to her mother. "Mom," she started to speak as she hugged her, but her throat closed up. Dixie held her close, rocking her slightly in her arms. Neither of them said anything, just sniffled and held on.

Eventually Dixie pulled back. She placed her hands gently on the sides of Tori's face. "I love you."

Neither one of them mentioned any of their struggles to get along over the years, the fights, the misunderstandings, the times Danny had to step in and negotiate peace. They just stood *together* for a moment.

"I love you." Tori poured her heart into the words, willing her mom to believe she meant it, no matter what.

"It's been a beautiful day," Dixie said. "Everything a young bride could want. You could treasure up these moments," her words began to trip over each other as she hurried to get them out, "and have a lovely June wedding. June is a beautiful—"

"Mom," Tori interrupted. She tried to stay calm. "A Christmas wedding is beautiful, too."

"Spring then," Dixie pressed. "I'm not asking you not to get married. Just let us get to know him better, make *sure* this will…"

Tori knew her mom was going to say, *make sure this will work.* She gave her credit for not finishing the sentence, at least. Danny had said more than once that it wasn't that they didn't trust Tori's ability to make sound decisions, but that a few weeks wasn't long enough to know if you could make a fifty-year life together.

Tori couldn't explain how, but she *did* know. "Mom, I appreciate your concern for me, but I'm marrying Joe on Wednesday." She was trying to decide if she should say more, press her case, but they'd been over this a dozen times.

Dixie took a deep breath and stepped back a step. "Okay," she said, wiping a finger below each eye, "go get dressed. Fix your makeup. Have fun and *be safe*. And keep Sammie safe," she added.

"I will, Mom. Don't spoil Ben too much." Tori wiped her eyes and turned to grab her bag and head for the ladies' room with the other girls. For all that her mom had been trying to get her to reconsider her rush to the altar, except for the last two minutes, today she was the epitome of support. Tori closed her eyes for a moment and willed herself to commit this day to memory. Hard to say how long this truce would last.

CHAPTER 5

JOE straightened his cuffs as he looked in the mirror. The alterations were perfect, no small feat for a man of his size. The last time he'd worn a tuxedo must've been the twins' weddings about four years ago. He was pleasantly surprised. Tori would probably like this look.

The tailor at the tuxedo shop made a few adjustments and stepped back again, eyeing Joe critically from every angle. He finally nodded his head. "Good."

Joe nodded back. "I'm sure my friends will be here any minute. Work must've kept them."

The man nodded and returned to his station behind the curtain.

All of the Paladins in the various sectors of the city were taking shifts to patrol their own neighborhoods as well as to provide backup when one of them had a holiday event, or to give added protection to the worst areas of the city. Stretch's team agreed to cover Joe's team's area during Joe's wedding, and an older team offered to cover tonight when many of Joe's friends would be at his bachelor party.

That didn't explain where his non-superhero brother Carl was, though. Joe looked at his watch. Right as someone punched him hard in the arm. Joe turned to see his big brother coming in for another swing. They traded a few punches and fell into a backslapping hug that would've felled smaller men.

The sharp sound of a clearing throat cut short their greeting.

The tailor stood nearly a foot shorter than Joe, and must be easily sixty pounds lighter. But he had the same commanding presence as Joe's old high school principal, Mr. Granger. Carl must've sensed it as well because he, too, stood up straight, hands to himself.

Joe whispered to his brother, "You're late."

"Kids," Carl whispered back. "You can't make them listen and you can't trade them in."

Joe snickered. When the tailor raised his eyebrow, Joe put on a more serious expression. Apparently, grooms were supposed to act more mature. He stood waiting for the tailor to tell him what to do.

The tailor appeared to be waiting for Joe to do something. He finally swished his hand at Joe. "You may take that off now. *Carefully.*"

The rest of the men in the bridal party — Bull Kincaid, Mickey Valient, and Darian Johnson — all walked in together a few minutes later as the tailor adjusted Carl's trousers.

"Hey, guys!" Joe called. "Where ya been?" He pointed to his watch. "Another time zone?"

Joe saw the tailor give Carl a menacing glare for waving. He stepped back. Safer to stand over here with his friends. "Hey, you guys better hurry," he said quietly, shaking hands and doing fist bumps. "The little guy is getting perturbed."

The men started toward the back room to find their tuxedos. Another loud throat-clearing stopped them in their tracks. That tailor could say more without saying anything. Joe tried not to smile.

While Carl's tuxedo was tweaked—"What have you been eating?" Joe heard the tailor ask his brother—Joe asked the others about work.

"Aw, man," said Darian, "there were *five* muggings in Memorial Park last night. And those are just the ones that got away."

"What happened?" Joe asked.

"Christmas party," said Mickey with a scowl.

Joe frowned.

"Sector Eight had a team Christmas party," Bull explained, "and J-Mac forgot to tell his Sector One team that they were to cover for them."

"Irresponsible." Mickey shook his head. "Someone could've been hurt."

"But they weren't," Darian said soothingly. "We can't be everywhere, neither can the police. One starfish at a time, buddy." Darian slapped Mickey's shoulder. "Who's covering for us tonight?"

"Sector Eight," Mickey grumbled.

Joe and Bull grinned at Mickey's fresh scowl. The man was a perfectionist in the worst way, and a tough team leader as Tick Tock. But the three of them and Hayley Addison worked well together keeping Sector Seven safe from the worst of Double Bay's crooks and criminals.

Darian slapped Mickey's back and gave him a reassuring smile. He was a glass-mostly-full kind of guy and loved to compare their superhero work with the story about a guy saving starfish on a beach — we can't save them all, but we can help as many as we can. Joe liked his attitude. Too bad he served with Sector Four. It would be fun to work together more often than just the high-crime Christmas season.

The tailor, finished with Carl, brought over three garment bags, handing them to each man without asking for names. Joe didn't know how he could remember so many people's names and faces. Must be a gift.

The man stared up at Darian. "I know your face, but the name isn't right. You are related to Cesar Johnson, yes? Michigan Wolverines basketball?"

Darian grinned. "He's my little brother."

The tailor actually smiled. "Excellent player. How is his knee?"

"He's walking again. Beat the odds. Got hired a few months ago by a high school south of Ann Arbor to teach English and coach basketball."

The tailor beamed at Darian and clasped his arm briefly.

"That is wonderful news. Blessings on your family." Then the stern expression returned. "Now dress, all of you." He swished his hand toward the curtained area.

In between the trying on, the final adjustments, and the tailor letting out a button on Carl's tuxedo jacket—"No more cookies until *after* the wedding," scolded the tailor—Joe told the guys about the morning's terrifying events.

"There I was, staring Tori's dad, Danny Lewis, in the eye — *as Superhero X*!" Joe wiped his hand across his eyes. "What if he recognized me?"

"Did he?" asked Carl.

Joe shrugged. "I don't know. But if he says something to Tori…"

"I was there, man," said Darian, "and the guy had the same shell-shocked expression everybody does when they're being robbed. He didn't recognize you."

"I can't let any of her family know until she knows," Joe said. "I'm just saying, we've got to be careful."

"So tell her, already," said Mickey.

"I'm going to," Joe heard his voice rising with a defensive ring. "As soon as I'm sure she…that she…" He rubbed his chest, unsure how to put it in words.

"You want to be sure she loves you for you, *Joe*, before she has to decide what she thinks about X," Carl stated, as if it were obvious.

Joe glanced at him in surprise.

"I get it, brother," Carl said. "You want to make sure the glue has hardened before you have to test it."

Joe nodded. "But Dad's not…"

"He may be a superhero, but he's also a pastor with a whole other agenda of things he thinks are important. And he's our dad. You know he's gotta be feeling protective."

Joe raised his eyebrows. "No, actually, I hadn't thought of that. I thought he was acting tough as the head of the Paladin's Guild."

"That, too," Mickey said with a firm nod.

Carl clapped Joe on the back. "When you have kids, you'll understand. I'm beginning to get it now after thirteen years of being someone's dad. I think parents are always a little messed up in the head. There's more second-guessing going on up here," Carl tapped his temple, "than a squirrel trying to cross a four-lane road."

Carl was the only married one of the group. Even though he didn't have powers, Joe's oldest brother had always been a fount of wisdom in just about everything Joe had ever needed to learn. If Carl understood why Joe was feeling nervous about explaining his family to his fiancé, then Joe must not be completely out of line.

"Or you could not get married," Mickey said.

Joe glared at him.

"What? I'm just stating the obvious. I'm sure I'm not the only one thinking it." Mickey looked around at the others but no one would meet his eye.

"You love her, marry her," Bull said, folding his arms over his chest. "Everything else will work out."

Joe took a deep breath. "Okay, so tonight, we need to make sure no one gets too drunk and forgets that they're in public — or forgets that Tori's brother will be with us. Agreed?"

"Relax, man," Darian slapped his back. "It's just a bachelor party."

JOE'S friends had arranged for a private room at the back of a local sports bar. Most everyone had already arrived. Driving over had taken longer than usual because the long-awaited snow had finally started to fall. People were driving as if they couldn't remember what to do when the white stuff came down.

As Joe walked in, a loud chorus of yells and whistles and raucous cheering filled the air. The dark wood tables were already covered with pizzas, hot wings, chips and salsa, mozzarella sticks, and pitchers of beer. His younger brother Stuart and Tori's brother

Kevin stood at the door collecting car keys in empty French fry baskets.

Joe's friends came over, slapping him on the back, ribbing him about his rush to get married, and talking animatedly about the Notre Dame football game on one of the televisions. Joe saw basketball on another television, and his brother Eddie was up on a chair trying to change a golf channel on a third TV. A waitress in a short skirt laughingly told him to get down.

Yup, it was gonna be a good night.

Joe shucked his coat, took the beer his brother Eddie handed him, and grabbed a slice of pizza with everything. As soon as the Notre Dame game hit half-time, his friends crowded around the entrance to the room. Joe started to walk over to see what was going on, but Bull pulled him back.

"Hold on there, buddy." Bull grinned at him and folded his arms over his chest. "Just watch."

Music beat heavily from the direction of one of the food tables. A moment later, the crowd of men parted in a riot of whistles and calls. A beautiful young woman dressed in what appeared to be only a Norte Dame football jersey sauntered in toward Joe.

Darian pulled up a chair in the center of the room and several hands forced Joe to sit. He groaned and laughed and didn't put up too much of a protest.

The girl danced around him for a minute, then began pulling off her jersey. Joe assumed she must have something on underneath since it was a public place, but he wasn't prepared for the University of Michigan cheerleader uniform. The hooting and hollering got louder. He hoped the Wolverine fans wouldn't start knocking around the rival Fighting Irish fans.

The girl had fantastic abs. The thought had barely formed when she did a backwards flip in front of him. She broke into a suggestive cheer that fit the occasion and proceeded to shimmy and shake in a most delightful way.

Suddenly some guy Joe didn't know reached out and grabbed at her. She was in the middle of a cheerleading move so he didn't

get a good hold before she jumped away.

Joe was out of his chair a second later, but two of his friends had already gotten between the newcomer and the dancer.

The guy called out something crass. Obviously drunk, if the slurring and smell were any indication.

"This is a private party," Carl said, reaching his hand out to turn the guy toward the door.

"Get your hands off me," the guy's voice got ugly and he pushed Carl.

Joe stepped up just as a few more unknowns broke through the crowded doorway. "Now that's enough," he said firmly.

Eddie stepped to Carl's other side. The three brothers were lumberjack-huge, Hannah always said. Joe knew they made an imposing barrier.

Apparently not imposing enough for the heavily inebriated. One of drunk #1's cohorts swung at Eddie who easily ducked. Darian, behind him, didn't see the swing coming until it almost landed. He moved enough to take it on the shoulder. As he spun, Darian swung his leg out wide to trip the guy.

As in, swung his leg *way* out. Not all of his friends were superheroes, and Joe didn't want anyone — especially Tori's brother — asking questions about strange things they thought they saw. He needed to stop this *now*.

"No, guys, let's just—" That was all he got out.

He ducked a punch and looked around for the girl. She was safely surrounded by the younger brothers and Mickey. Though Mickey was rolling up his sleeves.

He saw Bull pick up one of the drunks and haul him out of the room in a fireman's carry. If there had been a snowbank, he was sure his friend would've happily dropped the guy into it. For all that Bull was huge and stronger than any normal man, he was a bit of a pacifist.

Not so for most of the rest of Joe's friends, if prevailing activity counted for anything. One of his friends grinned as he ducked a punch and threw his own.

Joe turned to ask Carl to help him carry the drunkards outside. He walked right into a punch in the jaw. Ow. His strength came from absorbing the tensile strength of any metal he touched. Unfortunately, he wasn't wearing any metal right now. So much for off-duty.

The moment of pain destroyed his good intentions. Joe grabbed the guy in a chokehold and pulled one of his arms behind his back till he cried out. Then he walked the guy out of the bar.

Well, Joe walked. Drunk #3 couldn't quite keep his legs under him. The bar's security man met Joe outside, giving Joe a brusque nod as he let the drunk fall to the ground.

By the time he walked back into the private room, the ruckus was mostly over. The unwanted company had been cleared out, and half of the guys were already eating again.

"Not even a spilled beer," exclaimed one of Joe's normal friends with a grin. "Happy bachelor party, old man!"

Joe couldn't help but chuckle. He slapped his friend's back and walked over to where the dancer stood. Stuart and Kevin were obviously enjoying assuring her of her safety. They looked a little googly-eyed, in fact.

"I'm sorry about that," Joe said to her. "Are you okay?"

"I'm fine, thanks," she said. "A little more exciting than I thought it would get, though. I heard you're a preacher's kid. I figured this would be tame."

"You and your friends certainly know how to fight," added Kevin.

Joe ran one hand through his hair, feeling a little embarrassed and not sure how to respond.

"Even preacher's kids grow up to be strapping young men," Stuart said to the girl.

He must've realized how ridiculous that sounded right after the words came out of his mouth. He turned red and struggled to say something else, anything else. "Pizza?"

The girl bit her lip, smiled, and shook her head.

"Really," Joe said, thinking that sounded like a gentlemanly

thing to offer, "can we buy you dinner? Get you something to drink?"

"Um," she paused, looking around at the roomful of men yelling at TVs and eating and drinking with both hands. "Did you want me to finish?"

Joe smiled at her like he would have at one of his sisters' friends. "That's okay, you were great. Nice bit with the football rivalry."

She nodded toward Joe's friend, Tom, currently cheering on a play by the Irish. "Tom thought it would be funny."

Before Joe could respond, Kevin spoke up. "You want to hang out and watch the game? There's plenty of food."

She paused, considering, and Joe was certain Kevin would be shut down. Then she shrugged and nodded. "Sure."

She followed Kevin over to a pile of plates. Joe and Stuart watched for a moment as the two laughed at something, then looked up at the game and whooped.

Stuart shook his head. "During the fight, he told her he was pre-med."

Joe laughed. "Didn't I tell you? You need a sexier major than computer science. Hey, he didn't see anything, did he?"

"I thought you were supposed to tell her already?"

"I'm going to. But that doesn't mean her family is ever going to know. I'm pretty sure our secrets will have to keep forever where they're concerned."

Stuart shook his head. "I don't think he saw anything more than a bar brawl with some guys who know how to fight."

Joe nodded. "Thanks for taking care of things over here."

Stuart shrugged. Then he looked up at Joe and grinned. "You gonna tell Mom if I have a beer tonight?" he asked. "We've got a line of cabs coming at eleven. We already arranged with the bar owner that everyone would pay twenty bucks for overnight parking."

"If I don't see anything, I won't have to lie." Joe hit his fist gently against his brother's arm. "Three more months and we'll give you a twenty-first birthday party to beat the band."

"Yeah?" They walked over to get some food. "There gonna be girls?"

CHAPTER 6

TORI and Lexie held tightly to Ben's wrists so his hands didn't slide out of his mittens. "One, two, three," they sang out, pulling him up high in the air and dropping him to his feet.

Close to four inches of snow had fallen last night, and all three of them wanted to walk to church this morning. Their breath puffed out into the cold air and their boots crunched on the snow. They swung Ben up in the air again. This time he didn't put his feet down so that he landed on his knees.

The equivalent of "Make a snow angel, Mommy," came out in his broken toddler English.

"No, Benji," Lexie scolded. "Stand up." She brushed the snow off his dark blue corduroys. "We can play in the snow at Grandma and Grandpa's. I don't want you to get wet before Sunday School."

After a minute, Ben complied, stomping his feet through the snow so it puffed up.

Tori kept thinking, I'm going to miss this. Then she had to remind herself, she would only live a few blocks farther away than she had before.

She smiled in the crisp morning air. What kind of magic was this — she wouldn't have to give up anything when she got married, and she was gaining the whole world.

Lexie looked over at her. "What are you smiling at?"

Tori grinned. "Isn't the world a beautiful place?"

Lexie shook her head and chuckled. "You're drunk on love."

Tori laughed out loud. "I know!"

"You're so lame." But her sister smiled when she said it.

"You know, you and Hayley and I made that no-men pact, but you two are the only people who aren't telling me what a terrible mistake I'm making." Tori had been waiting for one of them to say something. The suspense was killing her.

Lexie walked in silence for a moment or two. "It's possible, I suppose, that out of the three or four billion men on this planet, not all of them are irredeemable jerks."

Tori smiled. She knew Lexie tempered her language in front of Ben. What she meant was much worse.

"The older he gets," Lexie nodded to her son, "the more I see how I can help him learn to be a good man. Kind, honest, compassionate, responsible."

"Like Dad," Tori said.

Lexie glanced over and gave her a quick smile. "Yeah, like Dad. But hopefully with a little more backbone."

Tori didn't want to argue with her. She vacillated between thinking Dixie was a control-freak or Danny was a push-over. She didn't understand her parents' marriage.

But she sure appreciated Lexie's high praise — Joe fell into the category of "not an irredeemable jerk."

When they got to church, he was waiting for her by the front door. He pulled her in for a quick kiss, making her giggle. Then he crouched down and held up his hand to Ben.

Ben high-fived him and laughed.

"Morning, Joe. Come on, Ben, let's get your coat off," Lexie said.

"No!" Ben turned his back to his mom and held up his hands to Joe. "Off."

Joe laughed and pulled off the boy's mittens. "Ooo, you've got mittens on a string. You're so lucky."

Ben smiled at Joe and swung his arm, making his mitten fly around on the end of the cord it was attached to.

Joe made a game out of getting Ben's outerwear off, handing the pieces to Lexie. Then he tossed Ben up in the air a couple times

and airplaned him over to his mom.

Tori promised Lexie they'd save her a seat as her sister took Ben to Sunday School. She turned back to Joe. "You are so good with kids."

He shrugged. "'Cause I still am one." He leaned down and whispered in her ear, "Wanna go make out in my dad's office?"

Tori gasped and slapped his shoulder. "Joe!" she hissed. "We're in *church*."

He laughed. "I just wanted to see your expression. I can't tell if you're blushing since your cheeks are still red from the cold."

Probably. Everything he did made her blush. She wondered how long that would last. Hopefully, a long, long time.

Joe took her hand and led her from the cloakroom at the side of the narthex toward the sanctuary. But crossing a lobby never took longer. Tori figured *every single person* they tried to walk past stopped their conversation to congratulate them. She hugged at least a dozen people she didn't know.

By the eighth or ninth exuberant embrace from a stranger, her enthusiasm became forced. Her stomach started to feel a little hot and nervous. She hadn't felt this way in months. Apparently, she'd gotten all the hugs she could take at the bridal shower yesterday. She needed to stop soon before she did something embarrassing. Like tell everyone to back off.

Tori wondered if Princess Kate felt this way at her wedding.

Having successfully navigated the narthex, they stopped at almost every row inside the sanctuary. Good thing they had gotten here a little early. Tori saw Lexie walk by and wink, mouthing, "I'll save *you* a seat."

Tori smiled, then turned to hug another couple. At least these people she knew. "Thank you," she said yet again.

Tori and Joe joined Lexie a few rows from the front. While a guest pianist played some Christmas music off to the right, Joe whispered to her, "Have a good time last night?"

"Yes," Tori whispered back. "You?"

"Yeah. What'd you do?"

The pianist started playing *Greensleeves*.

"Oh, I love this song. We went to dinner, and we all wore little plastic tiaras. Mine said Bride." She flashed him a grin. "Then we went line dancing at a place on the UNM campus. Country music," she teased, and he made a face. "Very fun. We laughed so much my cheeks hurt."

"Dancing, huh?" Joe squeezed her hand. "Did you dance with anyone?"

Tori looked him in the eye and made a soft sound that she meant as, *I know what you're really asking and you're being silly.* But she said, "It's line dancing, Joe. You dance with everybody."

He raised his eyebrows. "Were the people you danced with good-looking?"

Tori giggled softly, trying not to draw attention. "Was the cheerleader at your party good-looking?" She raised her eyebrows in return.

"How did you know there was a cheerleader?"

"Because your very sweet brother who planned the party asked me if it would bother me."

"And you said?"

"No, as long as she kept her clothes on. So was she pretty?"

Joe grinned. "She was easy on the eyes." He raised her hand to his lips and kissed her knuckles. "Nothing like my girl, though."

Tori grinned and ducked her head. He said the sweetest things. She just loved that about him.

"Anyway, it was your brother who got her number, I think."

Tori glanced up in surprise. She was about to ask more questions, but the service began. More ammunition to tease Kevin with at lunch today.

A young family with three small children lit the Advent candles and read a passage about the birth of Jesus. The congregation sang "Angels We Have Heard on High," and Owen gave a lovely sermon about holding the joy and peace of Christmas in your heart all year. The service ended with a rousing rendition of "Joy to the World."

Tori sighed happily. "I love Christmas."

She pulled Lexie along as she and Joe faced another wave of well-wishers. If she had to meet every single person who went to this church, so did Lexie. Both of them were too used to keeping to themselves. It would probably do them good to get a little more connected here.

Even with all the chatting, they still had some time before they had to be at Mom and Dad's for Sunday brunch, so Joe and Tori walked Lexie and Ben home. That is, the adults walked. Ben rode piggy-back, played horsey, and pretended to be an airplane all the way home.

"Thank you for ruining him for me for the next month," Lexie complained. "I don't know why guys have all the strength and endurance when moms are the ones who really need it."

Joe chuckled as he swung Ben from his shoulders. "I love kids." Then he bent down and whispered in the boy's ear.

Lexie shot Tori an expectant look. Tori grinned and shook her head, sticking out her tongue at her sister. It was far, *far* too soon to think about having kids. They needed time on their own first. Though it was nice to see that Joe would almost certainly make a great dad. One day.

Tori gave her sister a hug, congratulated Ben on his snow angel, and waved goodbye. Lexie wanted to drive her own car to Mom and Dad's today since Tori and Joe would be going to Owen and Hannah's later. Back-to-back family get-togethers. She should probably get used to this.

Tori took Joe's hand as they walked back to the church. Joe had left his truck there this morning after he picked it up from the bar parking lot. As they walked back and then drove to her parents' house, they discussed wedding details.

Tuxedos — check.

Bridal gown and dresses — check.

Cake — Joe's Aunt Trudy said "check."

Luncheon — Hannah said "check."

Rehearsal dinner — check.

The church had a Christmas caroling event scheduled for 4:30

on Tuesday, and the bridal party had been invited to join them. The rehearsal dinner and rehearsal would follow. Tori was excited that so many family and friends had agreed to go caroling beforehand.

"This is going to be so fun," she gushed. "Much better than a June wedding. You can't go Christmas caroling in June."

Joe gave her a questioning look, then made a turn toward Tori's old neighborhood where her parents lived.

She rolled her eyes and sighed dramatically. "My mother once again pointed out the virtues of a summer wedding yesterday."

"Yeah, I'm still getting some of that from my side, too." Joe reached over and took her hand.

She squeezed it, and looked out at the neighborhood they were driving through. Her family had moved here when Mom was pregnant with Samantha. Dad had made partner at his law firm and they wanted to move to a better neighborhood. Tori had a vague recollection of their old neighborhood, and she'd thought it was nice, too. But Mom wanted to make Dad a proper lawyer's wife, and this house was better for entertaining. How many times had Tori heard that over the years?

She knew Mom and Dad loved each other, but sometimes she wondered if her mom was trying to prove something by being the perfect wife. And recently, Tori had been worried her mom thought Tori *wouldn't* make the perfect wife, and that's why she kept urging her to push back the date.

"Do you think I'll make a good wife?" she asked Joe now, still staring out the window at the big, beautiful houses in this well-to-do neighborhood. A neighborhood so unlike the one where she and Joe and Lexie lived.

Joe pulled over and put the truck in park. Tori glanced over in surprise.

"Neither one of us has any idea what our marriage is going to be like," Joe said, lacing their fingers together. "We both have ideas based on what we've seen in our parents' lives and our friends' lives, but we don't know how *you and I* will do it. I'd guess we'll have the fewest disappointments if we're willing to go with the flow a little.

"But I believe you and I will have a great marriage. You're honest and generous and loving, and you bring out the best in me. I hope I bring out the best in you. What other people think will only matter if we let it."

Tori felt her chin quiver. She undid her seat belt and slid over to him. He pulled her into his arms and held her tight.

"I think you're going to make a great wife, Tori." He pulled away. "I'd marry you today, if I could, but I'm willing to wait until Wednesday."

Tori laughed and felt the tears roll down her cheeks.

He wiped them away with his thumbs. "But I'll wait till June if it would make you happy."

Tori shook her head and wrapped her arms around him again. "No, I don't want to wait. You make me so happy." She pulled back enough to meet his gaze. "Not just happy, but…" She searched for a word to describe what she felt. "I feel strong when I'm with you. Strong and happy and peaceful and safe. But also, like I could do anything I set my mind to."

She tucked her chin down, feeling slightly foolish. She wasn't in the habit of sharing her deepest feelings with anyone, not even Lexie or Hayley. At least not like this.

Joe tilted her chin up and kissed her. At first, it was warm and reassuring. As it continued, it became a kiss of promise, and Tori reveled in it. Then it became a longing to end the waiting.

"Just in case I wasn't clear," Tori said when they pulled away, her eyes closed against Joe's cheek, feeling his heavy breathing in her ear, "I want to marry you *now*." She opened her eyes and said with a teasing grin, "But I'm willing to wait till Wednesday, if you are."

Joe grinned back at her. "I guess we could do that. Since we all have these nice clothes and everything."

Another laugh, another hug, another kiss cut short, and Joe pulled back onto the street.

Tori sat close to him, absorbing his strength. Together, they could do anything.

Even stand up to her mother.

JOE tried not to act nervous as he and Tori walked into her parents' house. He'd never been particularly uneasy about a girlfriend's parents in the past. But this was different. He hadn't met Danny and Dixie Lewis until the day he proposed to their daughter. Now, less than four weeks later, they were about to become a permanent part of his life.

His mother-in-law-to-be was intimidating, even if she was half his size. She may not have extraordinary powers, but she certainly wasn't powerless. When she looked at him, Joe felt like she was cataloging all of his strengths and weaknesses, and he wasn't sure which attributes were which around her. She brought out his best manners, his best posture, and more second-guessing than he'd experienced since he was a teenager.

Then there was the whole superhero thing. Dixie had made it plain at the first Sunday dinner he'd attended that she didn't believe in superheroes, thought everyone who professed to be one was mentally unbalanced, and that it was not acceptable subject matter in the Lewis household. Ever. Joe felt pretty confident she'd ban him from their house should the topic come up again.

Testing the waters, in this case, showed that they were indeed infested with crocodiles.

Tori's father, Danny, was much more easy-going. He was friendly and welcoming from the first, discussed Lions football and Red Wings hockey with Joe with enthusiasm, and acted like he genuinely liked Joe. But he'd also displayed that "I've been cleaning my shotgun in case I need it" look several times since Joe and Tori announced their engagement.

Joe had vented about all this to Mickey and Bull a couple weeks ago. Bad idea. Mickey told him he was a fool for getting involved with a girl whose family was so opposed to the idea of

superheroes. Some people have unusual gifts — were they opposed to chess prodigies as well? Mickey had been trying harder than anyone, including Tori's parents, to shut down this wedding. Joe didn't want to ask why. He might not want to know the answer.

Bull, ever the supportive friend and a true romantic, leaned heavily in the other direction. He eagerly performed the duties of best man, reminding Joe about expected gifts to the bride and bridal party, urging him to spend the extra money on the honeymoon package, and helping him get his house ready for his new bride. "Love changes everything," he insisted. It made Joe wonder why Bull and Hayley couldn't make things work.

But today was going to be even more difficult than usual. Today Joe had to pretend he hadn't seen Danny yesterday morning, hadn't saved him from a pair of armed muggers, and in fact didn't know anything about it. Would Danny bring it up? Did the family know? Tori hadn't said anything and he was sure she would have if she had known.

So probably Danny hadn't told anyone. Which was good. Joe wouldn't say anything and the whole situation would be a non-issue.

Unless Danny started thinking that Joe looked like the guy who helped him. And, darn it, Stretch had given their superhero names. No way to take that back. Granted, only the Paladins and the SLU knew Joe was Superhero X. But Joe already felt under the microscope with this family. And Danny was a lawyer. Didn't lawyers go around digging up facts? The SLU wouldn't tell him anything, if he found out about the SLU at all. It wasn't a secret, but they didn't advertise their presence.

Joe took a deep breath as he took off his coat and hung it up. He just had to act normal and no one would be the wiser.

Everyone called out their greetings, and Joe sank with relief onto the couch beside Kevin. A football game was on — the Lions versus the Bears — and all the men were in the living room. Football was safe. That's all they'd be talking about today.

"So, how was your bachelor party last night?" Danny asked.

Joe stuttered as he tried to decide what to say. What was appropriate to share with the protective father of the bride? Some of his friends had allowed their powers to show a little, but Kevin had been pretty focused on the cheerleader, oblivious to everything else. "It-it was good. Very low-key. Football and food, mostly." He tried to make it sound like nothing untoward had happened, nothing that would make him look like a bad choice for this man's daughter.

Danny raised his eyebrows. "No girls?"

"Uh, just one and she…" Joe looked to Kevin for help. What had he told his dad?

Kevin apparently didn't mind talking about her. "She's a cheerleader at UNM, Dad. We think we might've been in a chemistry lecture together."

He told his dad that Teresa was a junior like him, but she was in the Honors College, majoring in international finance.

Danny turned his focus to his son, listening to him go on and on about the girl, asking him questions and ribbing Kevin about his new crush. Joe all but groaned in relief.

Then the Lions scored and everyone's focus returned to the TV. Joe cheered a little too loudly, an outlet for his nervous energy. He had to get hold of himself. Act like it's a job, an undercover job. Darned if it wasn't.

Even after he told Tori, her family would probably never find out. Carl's in-laws didn't know. Of course, Carl himself had never gotten a power, and he was quite happy about that. Joe's next oldest brother Eddie wouldn't acknowledge his power, and Joe assumed his in-laws didn't know either.

Lexie and Ben arrived, and the little boy gave Joe something else to think about. Ben high-fived all the men, then climbed on Joe and used him as a jungle gym. A few more relatives showed up that Joe hadn't met yet. He was beginning to think he couldn't wait until Wednesday. The "why are you getting married so quickly?" looks were getting harder to ignore. He wanted to tell everyone, I did *not* get her pregnant.

When Dixie called everyone in to dinner, Joe could hardly believe what happened — all the men got up and filed into the dining room. The Lions were on a third down, two yards from the goal line. In the next sixty seconds, they could score and get ahead for the first time this game. Joe knew Danny and Kevin cared. They'd all been cheering together a moment ago. Wow, Dixie sure held the power in this house.

Danny left the TV on, but muted the sound. In the dining room, Joe noticed the TV wasn't visible to anyone from the table. He knew because he walked around the table looking for a seat with a view. This family was so unlike his own.

Tori took his hand and they sat down next to each other, a cousin on Tori's side and Grandma Lewis next to Joe.

Okay, you can do this.

Danny said grace, and various bowls and platters were passed around. Always to the right, Joe remembered this time. Maybe everyone would talk around him and he could get through the next hour or two by smiling and nodding.

"So explain to me, dear," said Grandma Lewis as she patted his hand, "why you feel like you need to get married so quickly."

Smiling and nodding probably wasn't going to work this time.

Joe's gaze darted around the table to find everyone listening, waiting for his answer. How could he get out of this quickly and politely? "Chastity," he finally said. They knew he was a preacher's kid. It was a good answer.

Tori choked on a sip of water. Her siblings and cousins all started to laugh, then quickly tried to hide it. Joe wasn't sure why that answer was funny, but by the strange reactions around the table, he wished he could take it back.

"We all know how you feel about virgin brides, Grandma," Lexie said with a cheeky grin. "At least one of your grandchildren is going to follow in your footsteps."

Grandma Lewis pursed her lips slightly at the laughter from the young people. Then she leaned around Joe. "Is that right, Tori? You'll be a virgin bride?"

Joe glanced down at Tori. He tried to send her a message — sorry, and could they please go home now? Under the table she squeezed his hand, but she didn't look at him. She leaned over to tell her grandmother, "Only until we get to the hotel, Grandma."

"Victoria Joy!" exclaimed Dixie.

"What?" Tori asked with an innocent smile. "I only have to wait until after the wedding, right? I'm waiting another seven hours after that."

"That's going above and beyond," one of her cousins said seriously. "Good for you."

Dixie sputtered at one end of the table. Joe noticed Danny chewing and trying not to smile at the other end.

"At least we don't live in one of those cultures," Kevin piped up, "where they consummate their vows during the reception with someone watching to make sure they do it right."

Dixie spiked her son with a quelling look.

Joe didn't look at anyone else, just stabbed a forkful of beans from his plate and chewed, trying to stay out of the line of fire. He wanted to laugh with the younger people, but the older adults weren't laughing. They mostly seemed irritated.

In his family, teasing was as natural as breathing, and everyone laughed. But the Lewis family was so serious when they were together. They seemed to be big fans of privacy, apparently thinking you shouldn't talk about or joke about anything remotely personal. If anyone had a reason to be careful and secretive, it was his superhero family. Didn't Tori's family trust each other enough to be relaxed and open when they were together?

Grandma Lewis patted Joe's hand again. "Well, then I give you my blessing, young man."

Joe desperately wanted to laugh, or at least grin, but he forked a bite of meat into his mouth and nodded to the woman. If he could keep his mouth shut for the rest of the meal, maybe he could keep from adding ammunition to the hundred and one reasons Tori's family cited for postponing the wedding.

A few minutes later, when Dixie was engaged in another

conversation at her end of the long table, Danny said, "So Joe, you work in security, right?"

Joe nodded. "Yes, sir."

"You're a security guard?" asked an aunt. "That can't pay very well." She sent a pointed look to Tori.

It wasn't that far from the truth, Joe supposed. "So to speak, yes, ma'am." Let her think what she wanted.

"Does your company do residential work or commercial work?" Danny asked.

"We do both, though we have more residential customers right now. It depends on the needs of the client."

"I see." Danny nodded. "So do you protect retail stores, strip malls, banks, that sort of thing?"

Joe stiffened. Did Danny recognize him? Or was he asking strictly from the security angle? "There is another company who nailed down most of the banks a few years ago. I think we might have a strip mall or two, and yes, we do individual retail stores. A little of everything."

"Security at the mall is atrocious," inserted the aunt with a contemptuous sniff. "I hope you're not a mall security guard."

"Joe isn't a security guard," Tori said firmly to her aunt. "He works with clients to create a security plan tailored for their needs. He has a dual degree in engineering and computer science. He's excellent at what he does and makes a fine living. He even owns his own house."

Joe stared at his girl with surprise. Apparently, she was a good listener. He barely remembered telling her some of that. He lifted her hand and kissed it.

She gazed up at him with that gorgeous smile of hers, then she leaned over and kissed his cheek. From what Joe had been able to tell, this was a huge and embarrassing display of public affection in the Lewis house. He felt his heart swell.

Danny cleared his throat.

Tori winked at Joe, dropped his hand, and went back to eating. Joe was still staring at her when her father spoke up.

"So banks have good security?" he asked. He looked a bit skeptical.

Joe could understand why. "I don't like to comment on other firms' work," he said. "It can be a difficult business, especially this time of year. Every time you upgrade your system, there's a criminal working on a way to get around it."

Danny nodded. "Makes sense."

Joe cut a piece of meat and chewed. Should he say any more? If he asked a direct question about the bank, or commented on muggings, it might push Danny to wonder why Joe asked just the right question. On the other hand, it was his job — his calling — to protect people, make them feel safer.

"If you're interested, I could take a look at your security system here, see if I have any suggestions for improvements."

Danny's expression cleared a little. "That'd be great. Let's talk later."

Joe nodded. Tori's family may not have warmed to him any more as a "security guard" than they had to conversations about superheroes. But maybe he could win them over one person at a time.

CHAPTER 7

TORI tried not to be disappointed. Yesterday was the perfect mother-daughter day. Dixie was everything a girl could want — supportive, loving, laughing and smiling with everyone at both the dress fitting and the shower.

Today, well, it almost seemed as if her mother needed to make up for yesterday. As if, for one day, she had forgotten how much she didn't want Tori to get married and be happy. Might she be so worried about appearances that she would pretend to be supportive in front of Joe's family? That didn't even make sense since his family would be happier if they moved back the date, too.

"Flo is right, you know," Dixie said in the kitchen after dinner. "We need to know if he makes enough money to support you. I don't know why I never asked before."

"Probably because it's none of your business," Tori said, scraping bits of food off plates into the trash. She wished she were a boy child so she could go hide in the living room and pretend to be excited about football. She couldn't remember Kevin ever having to help in the kitchen when they had company.

"It is their business," Aunt Flo interjected, taking the plates from Tori and loading the dishwasher. "They don't want to be supporting you years from now like George and I are with Jessie and her husband."

Tori prayed for patience. She would not play this game with them, especially with Joe right here in the house. And at Christmas! She ground her teeth to keep her mouth closed.

"That's so true," Dixie agreed with her sister. "And you don't want to turn out like Lexie, either," she added.

"Mom!" Tori looked through the kitchen door to make sure Lexie wasn't within earshot. "That's mean."

"But true," Aunt Flo said, shaking her head. "Two babies, one taken away, no husband." She made a tsk-tsk sound. "Your mother says that you said you aren't pregnant, but if you are, you definitely *should* get married this week. You can always get divorced after the baby is born. That way you won't shame your parents."

Tori wondered why Christmas was advertised as this beautiful, loving time of year when everyone put their issues on hold for a day. That had never been her experience. Since Aunt Flo and her family only visited at Christmas and during the summer festival season, those seemed to be the times when all the gossiping and nastiness came to the center.

Now that she was getting married, Tori decided she would be away on vacation during Aunt Flo's visits.

"There are too many things you don't know about him, Tori," said Aunt Flo. "And I'm not talking about does he snore, though that will definitely impact your future happiness. I'm talking about things like does he have a retirement plan, how does he vote, does he buy expensive man-toys without asking. A couple of weeks is not enough time to know if you'll be compatible, let alone if he can support you in the manner you deserve."

Be quiet. Don't speak. Think about something pleasant…like the plane that will take you away from this family in three days.

"See? You don't know, do you?" Aunt Flo nodded. "And what about his relatives? What do you know about them? When you marry a man, you marry his whole crazy family as well. You're going to have problems. Mark my words."

Tori shot her mother a glare — *make her stop or else*. Dixie didn't seem so bad when compared to her sister. Tori should be grateful for that small favor.

"You can never fully know another human being," Dixie said, "no matter how long you know them. And part of the fun of a good

relationship is getting to know them and all their idiosyncrasies. But you can do that while you're dating. That's what dating is for."

"Okay, I think the table is clear," Tori said, changing the subject. "Shall I find out who wants coffee?" She left before anyone answered.

In the living room, everyone was watching the Lions with varying degrees of excitement. Sam was only half-watching as she texted someone. One of their cousins read a book on her tablet.

"Who wants coffee?" Tori called out, then counted hands.

Her little brother grabbed her in a gentle headlock and kissed her temple. "Gonna miss you, sis."

She pretended to try to wrestle out of his grip in their usual play. "I'll only be gone a week. Then you can come over and we'll watch an NCIS marathon some weekend and eat until we can't move."

"You're on," Kevin said and pushed her away. Something happened on the TV, and he was off on a rant, yelling and jumping around.

Tori glanced at the screen, but she only saw a bunch of uniformed men wandering around hitting each other on the head or the back or the butt. She shook her head. She had never understood the draw of this game. She couldn't wait till spring. Baseball, that was a sport she enjoyed.

Back in the kitchen, she helped cut and serve pie while Lexie passed out coffee and other drinks to the family in the living room. When everyone had a plate of dessert, Dixie urged her sister to go relax. Tori took her slice of chocolate cream pie in an Oreo crust and headed for the living room.

"Tori, just a minute," Dixie said.

Aunt Flo raised her eyebrows at Tori and sauntered from the room.

Great.

Tori waited for her mom to speak. She tried as hard as she could not to have a combative look on her face, but she suspected she looked defensive, at best.

"I apologize for some of the things I said earlier." Dixie's gaze dropped to the kitchen towel in her hands, one finger tracing over the holly berries. "It's hard not to get carried away agreeing with everything your older sister says. Sometimes you say things or let her say things that you later regret."

Dixie looked up from the towel, and Tori could see she meant it.

"You have an older sister, and you are an older sister. You must know what I mean."

Tori nodded. Though personally, she didn't think she agreed with everything that came out of Lexie's mouth the way Dixie seemed to always agree with Flo. Something to be aware of in the future.

Dixie took a deep breath. "I'm trying to protect you. I love you, and I don't want to see you get hurt. You don't—"

"Mom, I don't need protecting anymore," Tori interrupted as gently as she could. "I've seen a lot more of life's dark side than almost any other 27-year-old I know. I can—"

"You *don't* know how bad it can be," Dixie insisted. She tried to keep her voice down. "You've seen a lot, but you have no idea what I've protected you from. You don't know what's out there in the world, how quickly things can go horribly wrong, *especially* with a new husband and—"

"But that's true for anyone, anywhere." Tori waved her arm toward the street. "Any of our neighbors could have their house burn down from a few sparks on their Christmas tree. Any of our friends could go to the doctor tomorrow and find out they have cancer. I appreciate that you want to take care of me, but you must know you can't keep me safe from every bad thing that can happen."

Dixie shook her head. "That's not what I mean."

"Then what *do* you mean?" Tori asked in exasperation, her stomach feeling queasy from arguing. "Tell me!"

Her mother's expression froze for a moment. Then she said, "Your father was a very bad man." Her voice had a dead quality to it, almost without emotion.

"You've said that before. But just because you had a bad marriage the first time doesn't mean—"

Dixie frowned, pulling her arms around herself and rubbing one shoulder. "Tori!" she snapped. "Are you still taking your medicine? Dr. Huntington's office told me you've missed two appointments this month. I know you've been busy planning the wedding, but you can't stop going to the doctor just because you're busy."

Tori closed her eyes and took a deep breath. Should she lie or tell the truth and have an even bigger fight?

"Everything is fine," she said. That was true. She felt great. Maybe a little weird sometimes, but that was no doubt what happened as drugs left your system.

"I want you to call the receptionist tomorrow and get an emergency appointment—"

"Mom—"

"—for tomorrow or Tuesday, before you leave town."

Tori opened her mouth but her mother interrupted.

"Promise me," she insisted. She moved her hand as though to touch Tori's shoulder, then she pulled back. "Promise me you'll take care of this."

Tori sighed. She would take care of herself, but in her own way. She was an intelligent adult. She'd researched the pros and cons of the medicines Dr. Huntington had prescribed. She'd researched the various disorders the shrink insisted she had. And she had been writing how she felt in her diary every day to track the changes.

One thing she could promise her mother was that she would take care of herself. "I promise," she said. It wasn't really a lie so much as it was sidestepping the specifics of Dixie's demand.

"When you have children of your own…" Dixie paused and shook her head. "Go eat your pie."

Dixie turned back to where she'd left a plate for herself. Tori watched her for a moment. When her mother picked up her fork, her hand shook so badly Tori could see it from across the room.

Feeling like she'd once again not only let down her mother but

somehow done something worse that she didn't understand, Tori picked up her plate and looked for a quiet corner.

She ended up in the window seat in her old room, now Sam's room. She pulled her feet up and stared out the window at the falling snow. She'd always fallen short of her mother's expectations and she'd never understood why.

Would she end up being a disappointment to Joe as well?

Maybe the rules she and Lexie had drawn up when Lex was pregnant with Ben were something to reconsider. No men. Keep everyone out. Protect themselves at all costs.

Fourteen years ago, when Lexie got pregnant at fifteen, their parents had insisted she give the baby up for adoption. It had nearly destroyed her. She'd been arrested several times for stalking the adoptive parents, and eventually she ended up living on the streets using who-knows-what to try to choke off her emotions. It had taken years for her to get her life together again. And it had scared Tori and Kevin and Samantha into trying to be perfectly well-behaved overachievers.

Well, Kevin and Sam were overachievers. Tori had been trying to help Lexie save herself since Tori was barely thirteen. She hadn't had much of a life outside of that mission. When Lexie got pregnant with Ben, Tori moved in. Add to that their pact not to date, and Tori had been focused on her sister and nephew most of her adult life.

But then she'd met Joe. He was practically a fairy tale hero. Tall and strong and good-looking with a big heart and an easy smile. The only "weird" thing about him, and she wished she could think of a different word, was how strong and courageous she felt around him. She not only felt safe, which is what she'd yearned for her whole life, but she felt like she was strong enough to keep other people safe, too.

She ate a bite of the chocolate pie. Her eyes closed for a moment. Her mom made the best pies.

Maybe that's part of why she wanted to be with him, to use that strength for the good of others. Tori had enjoyed helping Lexie

build a new life. She liked taking care of Ben. She simply liked helping people. Period. Maybe that's why she enjoyed her temp jobs — she knew she was helping people who needed it. Maybe how she felt with Joe made her want more of the same.

She sighed. Or maybe she didn't know the *why* of anything in her life.

She savored her pie while she watched the snow fall. She'd think about it later. She wanted to be in a good mood today. Her dad would call everyone in after the football game and they'd exchange presents since Tori and Joe would be in Florida on Christmas Day.

Tori smiled. That was a thought to put her back in a good mood. Disney World at Christmas as a bride.

Wow.

She finished her pie and watched the snow for another minute. Finally. She was beginning to wonder if they weren't going to have a white Christmas after all. The way it was piling up this afternoon, the kids might even have a snowman built in Joe's parents' yard by the time Joe and Tori arrived later.

Before Tori knew Joe or any of his family, she'd admired the various snowman scenes in Owen and Hannah's front yard each winter. She always wondered if the family who lived there was as fun as the silly snow statues suggested.

God, help me not to compare my family to someone else's, but to love them for who they are. And please let Joe and his family be truly as wonderful as they seem.

Tori took a big breath and left the room, determined to love each one of her family members the best she could.

At least for Christmas.

RUNNING and running. Monsters in the darkness. Chasing her. Running.

Mom screaming. Monsters in the dark.

A dark corner with a mirror. Hiding from the monsters. Looking in the mirror.

Monsters in the mirror.

She was the monster.

Tori fought against the monsters in the dream, fought to wake up, fought the darkness and the fear. She kicked and kicked, finally realizing only blankets trapped her legs.

She fumbled for the bedside lamp. Breathing heavily and blinking against the light, she told herself it was just a dream. There were no monsters in her room. No monster under the bed.

She began to cry and rolled into a ball on her side. She hadn't had that dream in years. What brought it back? Shivers ran down her spine.

Still crying, she reached for her phone. She texted Hayley, *you awake?*

Beginning to shiver, she pulled the covers back up and wrapped them tightly around her. She hated feeling so alone after a nightmare. She wanted to go get in bed with Lexie like they used to in bad times past, but Lexie had to go to work today. She shouldn't wake her.

God, help me not to feel so alone.

She opened the texting feature on her phone again. No reply from Hayley. Probably asleep at 3:49 a.m.

She stared at the list of names on the list of recent texts. She shouldn't wake him. Did he turn his phone to vibrate at night? Everyone did, right?

This is what Aunt Flo meant — she didn't know Joe well enough to know if he slept with his phone nearby, if he turned the ringer off at night or not, if he was a light enough sleeper to wake up at the ding of an incoming text.

Tori buried her new sobs in her pillow. She didn't want to wake her sister. Though she also hoped Lexie would miraculously hear her and come in and hold her until the fear left and the tears stopped.

She stopped crying enough to type a text to Joe, *you awake?*

Please be awake, she begged him from three-quarters of a mile away.

But no one answered. No one came. And she lay alone in her bed until she cried herself back to sleep.

When Tori awoke again, it was 8:52 a.m. She couldn't believe she'd slept so long. Thankfully, the last few hours held weird dreams, but not nightmares.

Her eyes felt gritty and her mouth was dry. She reached for the glass of water she always kept by the bed. As she drank, she heard the light whirring sound of her phone vibrating on a soft surface. It took a minute to figure out where it was coming from — under the covers. She'd fallen asleep with it in her hand.

She pressed the middle button and saw that she'd received texts from Hayley, Lexie, and Joe. She flopped against her pillow and read them, rubbing her sore eyes gently.

Lexie teased her for still being asleep, and wanted to know if Tori would be eating there tonight.

Joe apologized for being asleep when she texted him, asked if she was all right, and said he missed her and loved her.

Tori ran her finger over the words. She loved him, too. So much.

Another text from Hayley flashed in and Tori read four from her. The last one said, *Wake up sleepyhead, I'm walking to your door.*

A knock on the front door made her jump and then chuckle a little. She got up, pulled on her warm fluffy robe and sheepskin slippers, and let Hayley in.

"Aren't you supposed to be at work?"

"I called and asked Brie to hold down the fort. She is turning out to be the best employee I've ever hired."

Hayley stomped fresh snow from her boots, took off her outerwear and followed Tori into the kitchen.

"Hot chocolate?" Tori asked.

"Sure, or we could go out to breakfast, my treat," Hayley said.

Tori thought about it for a moment. It was the sort of fun, carefree activity she should be enjoying two days before her

wedding. "If you don't mind," she started to say, and then she started crying.

"Oh, Tori," Hayley said in the exact right tone of voice. She came over and wrapped Tori in a big hug. "What's wrong, sweetie?"

Tori tried to talk, but she couldn't. Images from her nightmare scuttered through her head. She shivered and hugged Hayley harder.

It took a minute for her to get hold of herself enough to tell Hayley about her nightmare. She couldn't say any more. She didn't want to tell her *why* she sometimes dreamed she was a monster. There were some secrets she kept close, even from Hayley, her best friend since elementary school.

It was only Dixie's lies and shaming that kept the truth of the shrink and meds from Hayley when she lived with Tori's family during their senior year of high school. The last thing Tori needed now was for Hayley to decide she was a freak and no longer worthy of friendship.

Hayley looked around and pulled a paper towel off the roll. She handed it to Tori and pushed her into a kitchen chair. Then she got another paper towel, wet it with warm water, and handed that to Tori as well.

"I'm sure this is perfectly normal nerves," Hayley assured her. "Remember how Sarah cried before she got married? And Margie told us that funny story of how she cried so hard the night before, she still had hiccups the next day at the wedding?"

Tori nodded and tried to chuckle. It came out more like a grunt. She gently wiped her face with the wet paper towel. That felt better.

"It was just a bad dream," Hayley continued. "Let me guess. You had a fight with your mom yesterday, and you ate way, *way* too much at both parents' houses."

Tori nodded.

Hayley got up and put some water in the electric kettle. "I told Bull to get you one of these for a wedding present," she said with a smile. She turned it on and rummaged through the tea canister.

"Then I told him if they were on sale, he could get me one for Christmas. I love this thing."

Tori smiled at her friend and patted her face with the dry paper towel. Hayley always made things seem not so bad. Of course, Tori's troubles weren't nearly as awful as the things Hayley had gone through, but Hayley hardly ever talked about her past and rarely complained.

Usually Tori did the same, but it seemed like everyone was stressing her out. "No hot chocolate?" she asked. It occurred to her that Hayley was heating water not milk.

Hayley turned, hand on hip, and raised her eyebrows. "You really think you need more sugar in your system right now?"

Tori giggled for real this time. Ah, that felt better.

"Aunt Flo said some terrible things yesterday and Mom didn't stop her."

Hayley shook her head and muttered something under her breath.

"Not just about me, but Lexie, too. Even about my cousin, Jessie."

The kettle button popped and Hayley poured hot water into both mugs. Then she covered each mug with a small plate.

"If I'd been there, I'm sure she wouldn't have left me out." Hayley pulled two eggs from the fridge, and got out a frying pan.

Tori raised an eyebrow wryly and nodded. Hayley became one of the family in more ways than one when she came to live with them. Aunt Flo had decided she was fair game, too.

Hayley cut holes in the middle of two pieces of bread, buttered both sides, and lay them in the frying pan. She cracked an egg into each hole, then checked the tea.

"I'm not really hungry," Tori said. All the bad dreams and crying had made her feel a little sick to her stomach. That reminded her of the queasy feeling she had arguing with her mom. She got up and took the mug of English Breakfast tea, and doctored it with milk and honey before sitting back down at the table.

"Your long silence is making me uncomfortable," she told

Hayley.

"Sorry." Hayley sent her a quick smile. "Just trying to figure out what to say that doesn't make things worse."

"Worse as in trying not to call my family members a-holes," Tori half-laughed, "or worse as in trying not to agree with everyone that I shouldn't get married right now?"

Hayley flipped the eggs and toast, and pulled two plates from the cabinet. She didn't smile.

Tori felt her stomach drop. Hayley didn't think she should get married either?

"Eggy in a basket for two," Hayley said, setting the plates down. She got two forks out of the drawer behind her and sat next to Tori. She took a bite of her breakfast, chewed, smiled, and swallowed. "I was so hungry. You know I can say the wrong thing when I'm cranky, and I was getting close to cranky-hungry."

Tori just stared at her, waiting for the bad news.

Hayley gestured. "Eat."

Tori sighed. "Talk."

Hayley looked down at her plate. "Okay, if you eat. You'll feel better."

Tori took a bite and closed her eyes for a moment. No one made eggy in a basket like Hayley. She took another bite. Maybe she did feel a little better.

"Pinky-swear honesty?"

Tori nodded. If her best friend couldn't be honest with her, how could she figure things out?

"Ever since you introduced me to Joe, I haven't stopped being shocked. I mean *shocked*, Tori," Hayley said. "How in the world did you two find each other? To only live a few blocks apart for years and then suddenly run into each other? And then, *bam*, you fall in love just like that. And then you decide to get married a few weeks later?"

Hayley shook her head and chewed another bite. "You two are like a romantic comedy. I kept waiting for the other shoe to fall, but it hasn't. And I'm beginning to think it won't."

Tori looked up, feeling hope wash away the sick feeling. "But Mom is positive things will be easier if we wait to get married. Do you think so?"

Hayley shrugged. "You know how we used to laugh at those old re-runs of *The Love Boat*, about how people would fall in love in seven days? Did you know Kelly's boyfriend's dad did that? Apparently, he and the woman he married two weeks after they met have been married for something like four years. So who's to say what's the right or wrong way to do this?"

Tori cut a corner of the toast and a piece of the middle of the egg and put them in her mouth together. It was true, no two courtship stories were the same.

"A couple weeks ago," she told Hayley, "Stacy who runs the youth group at church told me that when she and her husband Gary were dating, they broke up and got together again seven times in five years. Now they've been married for eleven years." She looked at Hayley and they both shrugged.

"So who's to say?" Hayley asked.

"But not everyone who gets together, stays together. What if my mom is right and things would be easier if we waited?"

"Not to put too fine a point on it, Tori," Hayley said, pointing her fork at Tori, "but I've seen you two together. You really think you can make it until next summer without giving in? And how are you going to feel about this magical love you have if you *do* end up moving the wedding date up because you're pregnant?"

Tori thought about Friday night. No matter how strongly she believed in her choice to wait, she wasn't sure she could make it six more months. "Not being able to keep our hands off each other isn't much of a good reason to get married."

Hayley tilted her head. "Is that why you're getting married?"

Tori shook her head firmly.

"So what's really bothering you?"

She thought about it for a moment. Thought about yesterday's conversations with various family members on both sides. Thought about her nightmare and the other bad dreams and what they

might mean.

She chose her words carefully, not wanting Hayley to know about the shrink and the meds any more than she wanted Joe to know. "What if there is something wrong with me? Something that would be bad for our relationship? What if our previous pinky-swear to never get married was wiser than we realized?"

Hayley finished her last bite of breakfast, staring at a space on the far wall. "I worry all the time that we're broken, permanently broken, you and me and Lexie."

Tori nodded, running her fork lightly over the designs on the plate. That's why they'd made those promises years ago, and she and Lexie had renewed their vow to remain single when Lexie's boyfriend Rodney left her.

"So why do I feel this overwhelming certainty," she asked quietly, "that I can be whole again with Joe? It's not that I think I need him in order to be okay." She tried to find the right words. "It's more that when I'm around him, I feel like I can conquer the world. He's big and strong and he makes me feel safe, but *I* feel stronger around him. Even when I'm not around him, really. I feel like…I don't know how to say it…like I'm the *real me* when we're together. The "me" God had in mind when he made me. I feel beautiful and strong and confident."

Tori looked up to see if Hayley was terribly confused. But she was nodding. Still staring at the wall, Hayley said, "Funny, Joe said something almost just like that."

"What?" Tori gasped. "When? Where?"

Hayley turned to her and seemed to come out of her thoughts. She shrugged. "A couple weeks ago. I was with Bull, and Bull was with Joe, and…I don't know. It came up."

Hope soared. She and Joe both knew that their sudden, explosive love for each other was outside the norm. They'd talked about it enough to know that loving each other wasn't a problem. Liking each other wasn't a problem. Combining their two disparate lives and families seemed to be the real hurdle.

And he didn't even know about her mental health history.

Maybe that would prove to be the high bar on the hurdle that knocked them back.

"You know I haven't told him much about our past, me and Lexie's." As teenagers, Hayley had sometimes gone out into the city with Tori to look for Lexie after she'd given up baby Charlie and run away. "You think I should? Is it the kind of secret that needs to be told? Because I just don't see how anything good can come from the telling, or anything bad from not telling."

Hayley took their plates to the sink. "You know how I feel about secrets."

Tori nodded. "Don't tell if you don't have to." She thought about it some more. "But if I'm going to share my life with someone, am I being selfish by bringing secrets into the marriage? Am I being selfish by wanting to get married now instead of waiting?"

Hayley picked up her mug of peppermint tea. She liked it best when it was warm, not hot, having steeped for at least twenty minutes. She tested it, then took a few swallows, leaning against the counter.

"I think to be human in this broken world is to be selfish in many areas of your life," she said. "And I think there's a difference between selfishness and self-preservation."

Tori nodded, agreeing while also realizing she still didn't have an answer. Maybe subconsciously she thought that getting married now would help seal the success of Operation Freedom, her challenge to find her real self. Maybe that was selfish of her.

Or maybe all this pushback was the world's way of forcing her to really think about what she wanted, and to work for it, fight for it.

She thought about Joe. He was so wonderful. She would fight for him any day. She just didn't want to fight so hard that she hurt him, allowing him to marry someone who was so broken that he would be cut on the harsh edges.

Was keeping her secrets an act of selfishness or self-preservation?

And what she had worked for years to disprove, did she need to reconsider — was there really something wrong with her that

could hurt other people? If she was wrong and she did need to remain on medication and continue seeing a psychiatrist every week, there was no way she could keep that from a husband. And if she told him, she'd have to tell him that it had been going on for over twenty years.

What would he think of her then? Worse, if she found that she was right, and she didn't need the doctor and his drugs, but she'd told Joe about twenty years of medical "issues," would he ever look at her the same again?

A mistake like that could break the one thing in her life that was undamaged.

CHAPTER 8

BEING on vacation from MGV Security was not the same as being on vacation from work. Christmastime in Double Bay meant double-time for the superheroes who were willing. And because some weren't willing to work extra hard when they, too, wanted to be with their families, it meant you never knew when you were going to get another call for help.

Joe had barely woken up Monday morning when Mickey phoned. Of course, Joe told his friend he'd meet him at the clubhouse in forty minutes. He took a minute to reply to Tori's text from last night — wished, in fact, that he'd heard it come in so he could chat with her — then he threw on his super suit, put some cat food in Snickers' dish, and rushed out.

At the clubhouse, Mickey was waiting in the black SUV with dark tinted windows that they used when working. It was just the two of them this morning. Bull, a history teacher at Washington High School as his day job, wanted to visit one of his students at the juvenile detention center. Hayley, the fourth member of their team, had taken the week off so she could help Tori with wedding preparations.

Joe still couldn't believe Hayley and Tori had been best friends since elementary school. How odd it had been when Tori "introduced" them last month. Hayley had responded by saying he looked familiar, wasn't he one of Bull's friends, and Joe had gone along with it. From her reaction, Tori hadn't known Hayley was dating Bull either, which goes to show how scrupulously Hayley

protected her privacy.

Still, she had obviously kept Tori in the dark all this time about her secret identity as Green Thumb. Joe had only kept his secrets for a few weeks. That wasn't so bad.

"What's up?" Joe asked Mickey, buckling his seat belt.

Mickey pulled onto the street in the industrial neighborhood where their office, MGV Security — with the clubhouse in the basement — was located. "A church over on Wesley Avenue had just loaded a rental truck with over one hundred boxes of Christmas meals. Driver went inside to refill his coffee and the truck was gone when he came out."

"And the police are…"

Mickey slanted him a look. "Spread too thin. Still trying to work through the four car break-ins and two carjackings at the mall yesterday."

Joe nodded. Double Bay never had enough law enforcement to cover the city. That's why superheroes congregated here, plenty to do. Didn't hurt, of course, that despite the crime, the weather, and the unemployment, it was a beautiful place to live.

"Any ideas?"

Mickey didn't answer right away. He had some kind of crazy genius gift with technology, and he invented all kinds of gizmos that came in handy for their team, and for other superheroes as well. Over time, they'd also discovered that Mickey could often drive around, with no specific route in mind, and locate a vehicle he wanted to find.

It had happened accidentally several times when they were still in college. One day, Bull decided they would test Mickey and see what happened. Joe and Bull hid their cars in various parts of the city and asked Mickey to find them. Then they borrowed Joe's parents' cars and his sibling's cars, and then they rented a couple of big trucks. Still Mickey could discover the location of the vehicle in question.

So Joe didn't ask where they were going, just waited quietly in the passenger seat. He thought about Tori's text. Why was she

awake at three in the morning? She'd never texted him in the middle of the night before. He wished he had an excuse to see her before tonight, but she and Hayley were working on wedding stuff. He was vague on the details.

Joe noticed that the snowfall from yesterday and last night had accumulated about six inches on the ground, nearly a foot total. Not enough for Michigan people to be concerned with. Though as he was thinking about it, he noticed a few flakes coming down. He wondered how weird it would be to have a sunny and warm Christmas. This year would be his first, assuming the forecast for Orlando proved accurate.

That thought led to thoughts of Tori again. And her parents' conviction that the wedding should be postponed. His parents wouldn't be against that decision, either. His dad had gotten on his case again last night, asking if Joe had explained to Tori about their family.

Joe told him that he'd brought it up a couple times, but she didn't understand that he wasn't joking. He was working on it.

Owen hadn't been particularly happy with that answer. He'd lectured Joe about keeping secrets from one's spouse, the physical difficulty in running off to work at a moment's notice with believable excuses to one's spouse, the impossibility of explaining late nights, bruises, and missing or ripped clothes to one's spouse.

"If you don't want a spouse," Owen had said grimly, "now is the time to decide."

Joe told him he *did* want a wife and he *would* tell her when the timing was right. He was feeling kind of proud of himself for standing up to his dad without letting anger overrule reason.

Then his dad said, "If you don't tell her, I'm not marrying you."

Joe had stood there in the garage where Owen had ambushed him, staring at his dad and trying to decide if it was a bluff. He'd finally nodded his head and walked back into the kitchen.

He wondered now, as he watched the snow fall, how serious his dad was. Would he really stand there in front of the church and

Tori's family, holding up the wedding until Tori nodded her head and said she understood that Joe wasn't joking around?

Mickey mumbled under his breath.

Joe turned to look at him. "Close?"

"Maybe," he muttered.

They were in a residential neighborhood in the Park City area. The name implied a lovely little community, but it had long ago lost its luster. Today's Park City streets had as many thugs and boastful bandits as it had working class people trying to hold onto their integrity.

It was the "boastful" part that made it easy to find the bad guys here. Sure enough, Joe saw what must be the truck they were looking for a block away. People were pulling boxes out of the back and taking them to nearby homes and cars.

Mickey growled when he saw it. He braked for a moment and both men pulled their masked headpieces over their faces, adjusting the voice-disguising units at their throats and doing a sound check.

"Testing one-two-three," said Joe, now Superhero X.

"Dirtbags, scumbags, and thieves, oh my," said Mickey, now Tick Tock.

Tick Tock pulled the SUV to the other side of the street, grill to grill with the stolen truck, and tapped the other vehicle's bumper just enough to make the truck shake. Then he turned off the engine and jumped out.

Superhero X was already on the street, glaring at people carrying the stolen boxes of food. Most of them ran. Two lanky young men in flannel-lined coats and knit caps peered around from inside the back of the truck just as X and Tick Tock came around the sides.

One of the two started cursing up a storm, kicking and punching boxes in the truck. Apparently, he didn't think he'd get caught so quickly. Tick Tock bounded up into the back and pulled one of the guy's arms behind his back.

X followed the movement of the second guy. He stuffed a wad of cash in his jeans pocket and jumped out of the truck onto

the street, his legs already making a running motion as he hit the ground. X let him jump, afraid the guy would fall and hurt himself if X grabbed his leg.

But the guy forgot how slippery the street was now with the packed snow. He didn't get two steps before he fell on his face. X put a foot on the small of his back, using just enough pressure to keep him down.

He pressed a button on his wrist and called the police. Then he folded his arms and glared at the neighbors taking advantage of the situation.

A boy of maybe fourteen crept back slowly with his box. He made a wide circle, never taking his eyes off X. He stopped about twenty feet away and put the box on the snow-covered sidewalk.

"I didn't steal it," he said quietly. "I gave him all the money we had."

X let his glare soften a degree of two. "You understand that *they* stole it?"

The boy hung his head and nodded.

"I can see that you know it was wrong," X said sternly. He paused and then said, "So why'd you do it?"

The thief under his boot started spouting a string of curses and threats. X pressed his boot down harder until the man was gasping for breath.

"Well?" he asked the kid.

The boy shrugged. "We was hungry."

Well, hell. X sighed. The worst part about his job was that he couldn't help everybody. He couldn't solve all the problems. And he couldn't give this hungry child something that didn't belong to either of them.

All right, Lord, what can we do? We've got some hungry orphans and widows down here needing your provision.

The boy started to walk away, his head still hanging.

"Wait," X called. He remembered what Stretch spent his time doing when he was just Darian Johnson. "You know the East Side Youth Center? Near Overland Boulevard and Sixth?"

The kid looked up, hesitated, and nodded.

"Go over and ask for Darian. Tell him Superhero X sent you. He'll fix you up."

The kid furrowed his eyebrows, trying to find the catch. Then he nodded again.

"How much you give this thief?" X asked.

"Twenty bucks."

X bent down, dug the wad of cash out of the scumbag's front pocket, and started to peel off a twenty. The guy started fighting him so X pulled a zip tie out of a pocket and tied his hands. Then he picked up the money roll, pulled off the twenty, and stuffed the roll back in the guy's pocket.

He held the twenty-dollar bill out to the kid on the sidewalk. The kid took a step toward him, then stopped.

"Everybody makes mistakes," X said. "It's whether we learn from them that determines the kind of people we become. What are you going to do if this opportunity presents itself again?"

The boy looked at the scene around him — a stolen truck filled with boxes of Christmas food meant for other people; two superheroes standing on the thieves while waiting for the cops; neighbors watching from behind their curtains, hiding the boxes they'd bought so the superheroes wouldn't take them.

The boy turned back to X and said with all seriousness, "Cut the bologna into turkey shapes."

X burst out laughing. He almost fell over with his foot on the thief's back. He looked over at the truck and saw Tick Tock laughing, too, a rare sight indeed.

Darian's words came back to him suddenly. X couldn't help all the people in this neighborhood, or all the people on this street, but he could help one starfish.

"What's your name?" X asked.

"Jackson."

"How many people are going to be at your house on Christmas, Jackson?"

"Ten."

"All right, you're going to have all the makings for Christmas dinner for ten delivered to your house by tomorrow night. You know why?"

Jackson shrugged. "Because you're a superhero?"

X smiled at him. "Because I think you're a good kid trying to take care of your family, and I think you've learned something here today."

Jackson shrugged again. "Yeah, stealing's wrong, no matter who stole it."

"Exactly. And sometimes you get rewarded for being honest."

Jackson nodded. He scuffed the toe of his shoe against the snow on the sidewalk. "Can I shake your hand?"

X walked over to the boy and shook hands, giving him the twenty-dollar bill the kid had been too nervous to retrieve. Jackson pointed to his house and let X record him giving his address into the tiny microphone in the wrist of his suit.

When the thief on the ground struggled up as far as his knees, X told the boy he had to get back to work.

Eventually a patrol car arrived and the thieves were carted off. By then, someone from the church had arrived and, by some miracle, they were allowed to take the truck and deliver the remaining Christmas meals. One of the cops told the driver he'd call him later, see if the precinct could round up some more meals to make up for the missing ones.

By the time Tick Tock and X were back in their SUV and pulling away, X was feeling particularly good.

"I'm starving," he told Mickey after they stopped to pull their masks and headpieces off. "Where do you want to eat? My treat."

"Norm's burritos?"

"Done." Joe let out a contented sigh. "I love this job. That kid Jackson was a surprise, wasn't he?"

"I'll never think of bologna the same again."

"Too bad Bull wasn't here. He would've loved that kid."

"Good thing he wasn't. He would've taken him home with him."

Joe figured a lot of people had the Monday Morning Blues right now. They didn't like their job, wished they could be someplace else. But he wasn't one of them. He knew Mickey wasn't either. They couldn't be happier with the direction their lives were taking.

"If you go through with this wedding, how are you going to explain to her why you jumped out of bed so fast this morning?" Mickey was back at his new favorite subject.

Okay, so Mickey could be happier with the direction Joe's life was taking.

"Tori knows I work in security," Joe said patiently. "Some jobs have weird hours. She understands. And when she understands better, I'll explain everything to her and there won't be any more secrets."

"And you think hiding all your stuff at the clubhouse is a long-term solution?"

Joe was determined not to take offense at Mickey's grousing. He knew Mickey didn't care where Joe's super suit was, just that Joe could get to it when he needed it. And starting tomorrow, he needed to keep it at the clubhouse. No, Mickey's problem was with Tori's family.

"I won't need a long-term solution, Mick. I'm going to tell her. In my own time."

"So marry her after you tell her. If she thinks you're mentally unbalanced, you can still call it off."

"Why do I bother telling you anything if you're going to use it against me?" He never should have told Mickey what Tori's mother had said.

Mickey braked harder than he needed to at a yellow light turning red. He glared over at Joe. "Because I'm one of your best friends and my job is to protect you."

Joe sighed but it came out as more of a frustrated growl. With his elbow resting on the door, he rubbed his chin. How could he explain?

"You're afraid she won't love you if she knows who you are." Mickey stared at him as the idea dawned on him.

Joe started to protest. "She loves me, Mick."

A horn beeped behind them and Mickey accelerated. He sighed. "Joe, you've got a future already mapped out. The team can be without you for a week, but not forever. You gonna quit if she tells you to? What about your plan to work your way through the Paladins Guild and take over for your dad? You're the heir apparent, man! The Guild needs stability in leadership now more than ever. Are you sure you can offer that?"

Joe looked over at Mickey and frowned. "That is harsh, man."

Mickey shook his head. "Someone has to be harsh with you. You're not thinking. Guild leaders need to be able to see the big picture as well as all the tiny parts that make it up. They need to know their weaknesses so they can defend against them. This girl is your weakness."

"Her name is Tori. Not *she*, not *this girl*." Joe's plan not to get angry with his friend was reaching the breaking point.

"Maybe you two should hold on a little less tightly to each other and see what happens," Mickey said as he pulled into the drive-thru lane at Norm's. "Maybe you're both stronger than you think."

Both men put on their coats to cover their suits. No need for the cashier to guess who they were. Joe was trying to compose a reply when Mickey pulled up and placed their order for breakfast burritos.

Protect her.

The words didn't so much make themselves heard in Joe's head as they impressed themselves upon his mind. He'd been hearing them on and off since he met Tori, and he was convinced they referred to her.

Protect her.

Joe looked at his watch. It was barely ten in the morning. She couldn't be in danger. She was at home as far as he knew. Still, he couldn't shake the feeling that the voice came to him when she needed him.

He pulled his cell phone out of his coat pocket and dialed

Tori's cell.

"Tori's phone, Hayley speaking."

"Hayley, it's Joe. Where is Tori? Is she all right?"

"Hey, Joe. She's in the shower. Is something wrong?"

Joe didn't want to try to explain. He hadn't told anyone about the voice, afraid what it would sound like. On the other hand, he didn't want to ignore it either.

"Would you go check on her, please?"

"Um, sure, hold on."

Joe could hear in Hayley's voice what she thought of his request. But she was a professional Paladin and didn't argue.

She came back on the line a minute later. "She's fine," she said.

Was Hayley's voice strained? Was she hiding something from him? "Hayley, I'm serious. Is she absolutely okay?"

He heard Hayley take a deep breath. Then she said, "It's just pre-wedding jitters, Joe. She had a nightmare last night and it freaked her out. That's all."

Joe rubbed his forehead. She'd needed him last night and he hadn't been there for her. They weren't even married yet and he wasn't taking good enough care of her. Even as the thought crossed his mind, he suspected it was a little over the top. But he didn't care right now.

"Would you do me a favor? Would you go tell her I'm on the phone?"

"Joe, this phone isn't waterproof," Hayley half-laughed.

"Just tell her I called to see how she was doing, and..." He bit back his embarrassment. "Tell her I love her. Tell her, and then let me know if she said anything. I'll hang on."

Hayley laughed. Joe could hear a knock on a door, then Hayley's muffled voice. A minute later she was back on the line. "I never knew you were such a romantic, Mr. Clarke. I told her what you said, and I think you made her cry. She said to tell you 'I love you back.' Satisfied?"

Joe wanted to drive over and see her, hold her, make sure she really was fine. But he thought of Mickey's words — try holding on

less tightly. He'd give it a shot.

"Thanks, Hayley. Listen...be careful today, okay?"

She heard the worry in his voice and got serious. "You got it, boss. We'll see you tonight."

Joe started to say, I'm not your boss, but Hayley had already hung up. He took his burrito from Mickey and ate in silence.

He wished he knew what it meant, where the danger was, if there *was* any danger. Why else would he hear such a message? The first time he heard it was the night he met Tori, just after she was mugged on Halloween. That must mean that he heard it when there was some kind of danger, right?

"Everything okay?" Mickey asked.

"Just trying not to hold on so tight," Joe said, staring out the window at the falling snow.

His good mood had taken a beating. What if he was wrong and Tori wouldn't understand? What if the voice in his head meant that he was to protect Tori from *him*, from his life and calling? Or maybe he was to protect her by marrying her and keeping her close and safe. Now he wasn't sure.

He and Tori had decided to get married on Christmas Eve, not just because it was coming up quickly and they didn't want to wait, but because of what Christmas meant to them. It was a celebration of the moment God poured himself into human form to bring life and hope to the world.

To join their two lives into one on the eve of that celebration would be a symbol of the hope and love they shared as they started a new life together.

But maybe starting a new life with secrets, no matter the reason, would undermine everything they were trying to build.

CHAPTER 9

TUESDAY morning, Tori felt a little edgy as she drove Bill, her blue Honda, over to Joe's house. They had decided she would leave her car there, and tomorrow they would drive Joe's truck to the airport.

Assuming they got married tomorrow.

She did some deep breathing exercises as she drove so she wouldn't get a stress stomachache. One good thing about seeing Dr. Huntington for so many years, she'd learned a lot about staying calm. If she allowed herself to get too upset, her insides got all hot and tense.

They planned to meet Bull and Hayley at the mall for last minute Christmas shopping, but they would have a few minutes on the drive to talk in private. She still wasn't sure if she wanted to tell him about her supposed mental health problems, especially since she'd never felt better, but she needed to have the courage to at least have a conversation about secrets. After all, he'd sort of started a discussion on that topic at dinner Friday.

At Joe's, she saw his truck parked on the street as expected. She pulled into the recently shoveled driveway, up to the garage door. There would just barely be enough room for both vehicles when they lived there together.

Joe opened the front door before Tori could knock. He pulled her inside, kissing her before the door closed.

Tori felt the heat rise between them as he leaned her against the wall. Their lips and tongues and hands joined in a dance of

exquisite torment. She *did* want to marry him. How could she not?

He pressed against her and whispered in her ear, "I missed you."

She giggled breathlessly. "You just saw me last night." He kissed her deeply again, requiring a better answer. "I missed you, too," she admitted.

"Are you sure we have to go shopping?" he asked a minute later.

"It was your idea," she said with a laugh. "You're the one who asked Hayley and Bull to meet us at the mall."

Joe groaned and made a funny face. She'd begun to realize not long after they met that he did it on purpose so she would laugh.

"Besides," she teased, "you promised my grandma I'd be a virgin bride. We just have to make it one more day."

He kissed her one more time, this one gentle and loving rather than hot and lusty. "Then let's get outside in the cold."

Tori laughed. A meow sounded from above her head. Snickers sat curled up on top of the coat rack, blinking down at her. Tori reached up and stroked his head. He arched his neck and back and purred.

"We'll be back, Snicks," Joe said and gave the cat a good scratch. Then he opened the door for Tori and locked it behind them.

As she sat in the truck with the engine running, Joe brushing off a dusting of snow, she tried to order her thoughts. The Bible said not to let the sun go down on your anger, but she couldn't think of any advice about keeping secrets from your spouse. She wondered where secrets fell on the heavenly list of suggestions for better living.

Joe climbed in and off they went. The truck had better traction than her smaller car, but it slid a little on a patch of ice as Joe pulled into the street.

"Can I ask you something?" she began a few moments later. "I was thinking…everyone has things they don't want other people to know. Some of them aren't important, just embarrassing, like a boy

who wet the bed until he was seven. No one needs to know that. It doesn't help to know that about someone, and it certainly doesn't hurt anything to keep it to yourself, right?"

Joe nodded. "Agreed."

"So how do we know as a married couple, what is a 'bad' secret"—she made air quotes with her gloved fingers—"and what is just private?"

Joe made that grunting noise he always made when he was thinking. Tori thought it was rather adorable. See? She did know things about him.

"Funny," he said, "I've been thinking about that, too."

Tori looked over at him in surprise. "Really? Thoughts?"

"I don't know. Lately, I've been wondering…"

"Yeah?" Tori hoped they would find themselves in agreement on this topic. Then she would have nothing to feel guilty about.

"Some people think we're being selfish by, you know…"

"Getting married so quickly. Yeah, that's a word that came up in a conversation with me recently, too."

Joe reached over and squeezed her hand, then put both hands back on the wheel. Tori knew the roads were still slippery in spots, especially since the sun hadn't yet warmed the icier areas shaded by trees.

"So I'm wondering…" Tori knew she had to continue or she wouldn't be able to relax and enjoy their wedding. "For instance, do you think I have to tell you that in the second grade I got mad at a boy and gave him a bloody nose?"

Joe snorted a laugh. "Did you really?"

"Well, I wouldn't want to tell you if I thought it could change your opinion of me, so you answer first." She smiled when she said it, but she had thought half the night about what example she would use to test the waters.

"Honey, kids do that sort of stuff. It's part of being a kid."

"What if I told you that afterward I was told I had an anger management problem, and went to counseling?"

Joe raised his eyebrows and looked over at her. "I'd say that this

is probably the kind of thing you were asking about — something that would be embarrassing for you to tell me, and not at all important to our relationship."

Tori released a deep sigh in her head. Relief rushed through her and she felt her shoulders relax. *Thank you, God. Thank you, thank you. I don't want to do the wrong thing, but even Joe doesn't think we need to tell each other every awful detail of our lives before we met. Since I've been asking you for advice, I'm taking this as a sign.*

The street opened into more of a business area with fewer trees. The sun and traffic had melted most of the snow on the street so the asphalt was only wet, not icy. Joe took her hand again.

"What about other things," Joe asked, "things that aren't embarrassing childhood incidents? What do you think we need to tell each other before tomorrow?"

"The way everyone has been pushing us," Tori said, letting some of her frustration through, "it seems like *they* think we should tell each other everything. But I know a girl who went speed dating once, and she didn't like it. She said she learned more than she'd ever want to know on a first date. But later, she said, she realized some of that stuff wouldn't have bothered her if she was already into the guy."

Tori let Joe digest that before continuing.

"I can see that," he said, nodding.

"I've been best friends with Hayley since we were in second grade. We know *a lot* of each other's secrets, but we learned them over time, as the need came up to share, or as we trusted each other more. I'm sure we still don't know everything about each other."

Though that was something Tori really wanted to have the courage to change. Hayley often seemed shut off from the world, perpetually lonely even when she was laughing with girlfriends. Tori wanted to help her relax and enjoy life more. She just didn't know how.

"Part of me," Joe said slowly, "wants to tell everyone who has a problem with us that it's none of their business."

Tori nodded. Boy, did she feel the same way.

"But then I think about Solomon, the wisest man who ever lived, and his many advisors. He felt so strongly about it, he wrote several proverbs suggesting we all seek the advice of others. I don't want to be hard-headed and make things more difficult than they need to be."

"Yeah," Tori sighed. "That's crossed my mind, too."

Joe pulled into the mall parking lot and drove toward the entrance near Target where they were to meet Hayley and Bull.

Because of the way the snowplows cleaned the parking lot earlier, there were bigger spaces farther back from the doors.

"Mind walking a bit?" Joe asked. "My truck needs a bigger space."

"I don't mind. It's gorgeous out."

Joe pulled into a spot and killed the engine. Like Tori, he sat staring out the windshield.

"I don't want to be selfish—" they both said at the same time.

Then they laughed and unclipped their seat belts. Tori scooted over and Joe pulled her closer. That fabulous and overwhelming feeling of safety and strength encompassed Tori. They could get through anything together, she knew it.

"I love you—" they said together.

They both laughed again and Joe pulled her into a tight hug. "I don't want to do anything to hurt you," he said, the tone of his voice betraying the depth of his feelings.

"Ditto," Tori said, her throat too tight with emotion to say more.

They sat like that for a moment. Tori hoped these feelings lasted longer than the honeymoon phase like some people predicted. But it was more than infatuation or lust. It felt like friendship, partnership, the kind of thing that lasts.

Joe's cell phone went off. He saw it was Bull and answered it on speaker. "Yeah?"

"Get a room!" yelled Bull and Hayley. Laughter filtered through the phone.

"We saw you pull into a parking space two minutes ago," Bull

said. "There'll be plenty of time for hanky-panky in Disney World. Get in here."

Tori felt her face heat as she laughed. Being part of a couple was new and wonderful, but being part of a group of couples was more fun than she would've thought.

Joe hung up, then kissed her nose. "Finish this conversation later?"

"Sounds good," Tori agreed.

Joe pulled her out his side of the truck and held her dangling above the snow. Tori wrapped her arms around his neck, giggling at the strange feeling of hanging in the air. She still couldn't believe how strong he was. He kissed her soundly once more before he set her down and took her hand.

They met Hayley and Bull at the entrance, and the four of them made their first stop at Starbucks. Joe ordered Tori's hot chocolate exactly as she liked it, right down to the size she always chose. She smiled and wondered why people were so convinced they didn't know enough about each other to get married.

"Wipe that goofy look off your face before you embarrass us all," Hayley whispered in her ear.

Tori turned to her and grinned. They linked arms and walked over to where others were waiting for their drinks. "I'm so in love!" The words came out in a singsong whisper.

Hayley chuckled with her. "You're such a goofball. Listen, I have an idea. You know how we're going to split up after lunch, and you and I will get mani-pedi's while they do heaven knows what?"

Tori nodded.

"I saw a sign when we walked in that Victoria's Secret is having a sale. Let's go there after, okay?"

"Ooo," Tori clapped her hands twice, "yes, let's!" Hayley would probably buy something red or black like she always did. Those colors complemented her thick dark hair and creamy skin. Tori would have to walk past the cute flannel loungewear and buy something — gasp! — with lace. She could hardly wait.

The four of them spent the next couple hours shopping and

laughing. Joe asked her and Hayley's opinions on gifts for his sisters and nieces. Bull bought Hayley a red scarf with a green ivy pattern. Tori noticed a soft look pass between them. So sweet.

She couldn't remember the last time she had so much fun. The mall looked so beautiful draped in green and gold garlands with white candles and red bows. Lively Christmas music filled the air along with the smell of pretzels, cookies, chocolate — when they walked past the chocolatier — and scented candles. Tori wanted to look and taste and smell and buy a little of everything.

They shopped and talked and walked and laughed until they were hungry. Bull and Joe offered to take all the bags to their trucks while Tori and Hayley waited for a table to open up in the food court. The delicious aromas of pizza and Chinese food made Tori's stomach rumble.

They'd been waiting about ten minutes when her cell phone rang — Joe. Tori smiled and hit the talk button, noticing that Hayley's phone rang at the same time.

"You guys having a snowball fight or something?" she said. "The womenfolk are getting hungry."

"Tori, honey," Joe's voice was serious, "listen to me. The gang of thieves is back. I want you to stay in the mall, all right?"

"What? Well, wait, what are you going to do?" Tori stumbled over her words. Joe was outside with the gang of thieves? They were dangerous. He shouldn't be out there.

"Bull and I are going to try to help catch them," Joe said. "The police will be here any minute. Mall security is already—"

"Joe, no, you could get hurt! Come back inside and let the police take care of—"

"Listen," Joe interrupted. "Honey, listen, this is my job. You know that."

She bit her lip. Sure, but not the day before their wedding. What if he got hurt? He was big and strong, but it's not like he could stop a bullet. "But you don't work here," she protested. What if those men had guns? The reports all said they didn't, but what if they were getting bolder since they hadn't been caught?

"Do you want me to let other people get hurt?" Joe waited for her to answer.

"No," she finally said. If anyone could take down one or two of these thieves, it was Joe. And Bull was even bigger. So long as they stayed together, they could watch each other's backs.

"Do you trust me?"

"Yes." She didn't have to think about it. "I trust you."

"Then I'm going to help out here, and you finish up in there. Bull and I know what we're doing, we'll be fine." His voice was quick, tense, confident, and — for some strange reason — it gave her strength.

"Stay with Hayley," he continued. "She has keys to Bull's truck. We may be awhile if we have to make a police report. I'll see you tonight at church, okay?"

She took a deep breath. This was the first time she'd been with him when there'd been a situation he had to rush off to help with. It felt strange.

But she believed him when he said he could handle it. "Be safe," she said. "I love you."

After she hung up, she looked over at Hayley. Her friend spoke quietly into her phone, glanced up at Tori and nodded, and a moment later hung up.

"Soo…" Tori said. "This is a new experience for me. Happen often?"

Hayley shrugged. "Yeah." She put her arm around Tori and gave her a hug. "Don't worry, Tori. They know what they're doing. No one has ever hurt them. If you're going to worry about someone, worry about the punks who are about to get their asses kicked." She grinned.

Tori gave a little laugh. "Okay, I guess I'm following your lead."

What an unusual twist her life had taken. On the one hand, the current situation was a shock and she didn't know how to respond. On the other hand, it didn't surprise her one bit that if she were going to fall in love, it would be with a man who was a protector.

What did he say he was — six-five? Joe was huge, and the

strongest man she'd ever met. She doubted he'd get into it with anyone near his size.

Nonetheless, she prayed, *God, please keep him safe.*

JOE hung up the phone with Tori, then spoke to Hayley for a moment on Bull's phone. "Stay inside. Don't let her out of your sight. No, Mickey will be here soon. We'll be okay without you. Enjoy your foot massage." He laughed at Hayley's response and hung up.

Bull flexed his shoulders. "I was tired of shopping anyway."

Joe grinned. "Same here. So how do you want to handle this?" He pulled his warm knit cap out of a pocket and pulled it on.

"Thorn in the side until backup arrives?" Bull pulled his hat on as well.

"Love it."

The two men split up, keeping their eyes on the men and vehicles that had caught their attention a few minutes earlier. The SLU had briefed the teams with what information the police had been able to gather from past victims and witnesses.

The two- and three-man teams included a point man who would walk the parking lot looking like he was heading to his car or like he'd forgotten where he parked. He'd try to cross paths with someone with a lot of bags opening their car door or trunk. If the catch looked good, he'd grab all the bags while the second man pulled up in the getaway car. They'd load the car and take off, sometimes picking up the haul from a second point man.

Descriptions of the vehicles varied, so police figured they drove off-site to unload and came back with a different car. It seemed that each team tried to make two to three runs before they quit for the day.

Joe had spotted the first man while taking his and Tori's bags to his truck. The man's gaze darted around, always coming back

to face forward as he walked toward the far end of the lot. But the man was noticing people, not cars, and not people going *in* the mall.

Joe walked back up to where Bull had found a parking space closer to the mall entrance, told him what he'd seen, and Bull pointed to a car two aisles away. Dirty nondescript sedan, dark windows, looking like it was waiting for a space to open up.

Now the two of them started walking, Joe toward the man he'd seen, Bull toward the idling car.

Joe didn't want to scare the guys off, not with backup on the way. He wanted to surround and catch them, take down the whole team. But he also wanted to keep the locals from getting hurt or robbed.

A woman with more bags than she could easily carry exited the mall and walked down the aisle to Joe's left. Joe looked for the man he'd seen earlier. There. And on a collision course with the woman.

Joe walked toward them, trying to guess where the woman was headed. The green Explorer? No. The red Honda? Maybe. No. Just as she slowed near a white Mercedes, the handle of one of the bags ripped. The other man started jogging toward her.

Closer by a couple car lengths, Joe arrived first. Trying not to scare her, he said quietly, "Ma'am, get in your car."

She looked up, still struggling with her packages. "I don't need any help, thank you." She tried to get everything back in her hands.

The other man jogged up. "Let me help you with those," he said in a smooth, honeyed voice.

Joe stepped between them. "I don't think so. Ma'am, get in your car, please."

"OMG! OMG! You're the robbers!" She struggled frantically with her bags causing another one to rip open. "Leave me alone!"

While Joe was processing the fact that the young woman actually spoke in acronyms, the other man stepped around him. In a reassuring voice, he said, "Don't worry, I'm part of the community watch. We're patrolling the parking lots to make sure no one gets

hurt. Is this man bothering you?"

"Yes!" The woman shouted. "Help me!"

The man reached for her bags and grabbed one before Joe lifted him off his feet.

"Give it back to her," Joe commanded.

The man's eyes widened in alarm as Joe lifted him over his head. Joe gave him a shake, but the guy didn't drop the bag. He turned at the sound of a car's engine.

The car Bull was tracking pulled up, but Bull wasn't in sight. The driver slid out and grabbed several of the young woman's bags. She screamed and pulled. The bags ripped open, littering the snow with gaily wrapped gifts. The driver started grabbing and tossing.

Just as Joe reached for the driver, the first man kicked at his groin. Joe groaned and twisted, grateful it hadn't been a direct hit. He let the guy drop, hoping he'd get the breath knocked out of him. He reached for the driver, but the young woman started hitting him with her purse.

"Lady, *get in your car!*" He was tempted to let her get robbed. He hadn't experienced this kind of abuse in months.

The driver threw another bag in the front seat. As he reached for another, Joe clotheslined him. Wham! And down. He grabbed the keys from the ignition and tossed them a few car lengths away.

The other man began to stir, crawling toward the car. Joe picked him up, opened the rear door and tossed him in. Then he tossed the driver into the front seat and slammed the door.

Keeping his back to the screamer still whacking him with her purse — what did she have in there? — Joe placed his hands on the doorframes and focused. Then he squeezed. The metal crumpled in his hands like aluminum foil. With one hand firmly on the metal of the car, he hit his other fist into the door handles, then went around and did the same on the other side.

The perps weren't going anywhere. Neither the doors nor the windows were going to open now.

He turned to the woman who followed him around to the other side of the car, still screaming and trying to hit him with

her purse. "Call the police," he told her. "Tell them exactly where you're located and wait for them here. They'll get your packages back."

Not waiting for a thank-you he knew would never come, Joe took off across the parking lot. Without his costume, the police wouldn't know who he was. And he wanted to protect his real identity as much as he could from any officers not in the SLU.

He jogged to another section of the huge parking lot, his lungs burning a little in the cold air. He looked around for Bull, or anyone who looked like they were getting robbed.

A minute later he thought he saw Bull several aisles away. Joe jogged closer. Then he laughed. Bull was helping a little old lady into her ancient Cadillac. Joe watched him wait until she was buckled in, then he closed the door gently. He used his gloved hand to wipe the snow from all the windows and taillights. Then he stood out in the aisle, held up one hand to an oncoming car, and used his other hand to motion the woman to back up.

When she was safely out, she pulled up so the other car could have her space, then she rolled down her window. She spoke to Bull for a moment, he laughed, and she pulled away.

Joe walked up as Bull was waving goodbye. "What is it with you and kids and old people?" he asked, shaking his head. "A young woman in a Mercedes was beating me with her purse while the thief kicked me in the jewels."

A laugh burst out of Bull's throat. "Oh man, you all right?"

"I would've been better if I'd been holding onto the metal car," Joe said wryly.

"Aw, buddy, you and Mickey gotta keep working on those titanium-lined gloves."

Joe grunted and nodded. They walked down the aisle, looking for more thugs. "How do you keep yourself safe? Don't tell me no one's ever kicked you there?"

"Cup," Bull said.

Joe raised his eyebrows. "Every day? Even when we're not officially working?"

Bull snorted. "At Christmas, we're always working, aren't we? And it's not so bad, you get used to it."

"Better than the alternative, I guess," Joe said, stepping sideways and trying to rub his thigh unobtrusively.

It only took them a few minutes to find the next team. By the time they ran over and tried to stop them, both thieves had already gotten in the car. The sedan slipped and slid as the driver hit the gas.

"Light pole," Bull called and pointed.

Joe nodded and they both ran as fast as they could, angling to intersect with the car near the end of the aisle. Both men slammed into the sedan as the driver tried to turn onto the outer drive.

The car slid sideways. Joe and Bull hung on as it spun from the force of the collision. Near the light pole, they both sank their feet into the packed snow and pushed. The angle was perfect — the car smashed into the light pole nose first. The engine clunked and clicked and died.

The two men made short work of sealing the two thugs inside. They high-fived. Joe enjoyed his work most of the time, but it was particularly fun when they were winning. The adrenaline rush wasn't bad either.

In the distance, a police car headed their way around the outer drive. Both men pulled their hats down and walked nonchalantly toward the closest mall entrance.

"That's two," Bull said. "How many more do you think there are?"

Joe shrugged. "At least one more, I'd say. Let's call Tick Tock, see if he's here." He pulled out his cell phone and hit the speed dial for "Pizza Delivery," which was really the communication system in their super suits.

"Tick Tock, it's X and Powerhouse. You at the mall yet?" Joe nodded and shut the phone. "The entrance where the carousel is," he told Bull. "What's the closest way to get there?"

"Behind us, where the cops are," said Bull. Then he looked around to orient himself. "But if we go through the department

store here, we can cut through the mall."

The men rushed in, taking off their coats and hats as if they were regular shoppers. They took ground-eating but unhurried-looking strides through the women's wear and cosmetics sections, across the mall to the carousel going round and round with its music and horses, and back out to the parking lot.

Upon exiting, both men once again donned their winter outerwear to walk unnoticed amongst the mall's patrons. It only took a moment for them to find Tick Tock. He stood in his suit in front of another dirty older sedan, fighting with another man. As Joe and Bull jogged up, Joe noticed the engine making an awful noise. Tick Tock could use his gift to destroy machinery as easily as to create or repair it.

Bull picked up the man taking a swing at Tick Tock. Joe ran toward another man sneaking up behind the superhero. He tackled him, punched him once in the jaw, and left him knocked cold in the snow.

Joe dusted the snow off his knees and grinned at his friends. "What a day, huh?"

"Behind you!" Bull ran forward as Joe turned.

Another sedan sped toward them down the aisle. The three men worked together to stop the car before it ran over people, including themselves.

Joe and Bull ran toward the car, giving themselves space to slow it down before it hit the barely idling car directly behind them. Off to the side, Tick Tock threw his arm out toward the moving vehicle and focused.

The engine began rattling before the car got to Joe and Bull. The acceleration had dropped off, but it still hit the men with force.

Not as much force as Bull hit the car, though. Joe threw both hands onto the metal hood, felt the cold, hard energy rush through his body, and let his feet slide on the snow for a few yards. Then he and Bull both pressed their feet more solidly against the snow-packed asphalt.

The ragged sound coming from the engine gave Joe confidence

they'd stop the car without any problem. Then he looked behind him. They were still closing in too fast on the car Tick Tock had disabled.

He reached one hand behind him, turning his body sideways. Bull saw him and imitated his movements. Tick Tock shouted to the shoppers walking down the aisle toward them. One teenage girl was talking on her phone and not paying any attention.

Joe and Bull braced for impact. Tick Tock ran toward the girl.

Bam!

Joe felt his teeth clatter together as the bone-jarring impact rippled through his body. But his power protected him, and he didn't get pinned between the vehicles. The cars slid several yards on the snowpack before he and Bull stopped them.

Joe looked up to make sure all the pedestrians were safe. He saw Tick Tock with the shocked teenager between two parked cars. He turned to trap the passenger into the car the way he had the others.

Thwack!

Joe heard a loud crack and felt a blazing pain burst from his hip down his leg.

He hit the ground hard, remembering at the last moment how to land without hurting himself more. He realized his eyes were closed against the pain. Training and instinct pushed him to open them, looking for his attacker to strike again.

A lug wrench swung inches from his face when Joe reached out with both hands and gripped it hard.

A battle cry burst forth as his body reacted to the steel against his hands. He felt his muscles instantly gain strength equal to the metal, felt his skin tighten, and the pain in his leg lessen.

Joe jerked the lug wrench to the left, pulling his attacker off his feet. He rolled on top of him and pressed the X-shaped bar against the other man's chest. With the intense pain in his hip and leg, it was all he could do to remember not to press down so hard that he might break the man's ribs.

The man kicked and punched at Joe, but to no avail. Joe knew

hitting him now was like hitting a metal statue. The man probably broke a couple knuckles before he realized he couldn't fight back.

Joe heard sirens, shouting, and in a minute — it felt like ten — a police officer pulled Joe off the other guy. Joe fell onto his back again, squeezing the lug wrench in his fists.

This did not sit well with the police officer who put his hand on his holstered gun and yelled for Joe to drop the weapon.

But Joe couldn't drop it. The power coursing through him from the metal tool was the only thing keeping him from screaming in agony.

A moment later, Tick Tock knelt next to him. Joe heard him tell the officer to cuff the other man, that he'd take care of this one.

"Joe, talk to me, brother."

Joe gritted his teeth, trying to squeeze the metal harder. He focused on the steel. His body's reaction to metal was instant and all-encompassing. The incredible healing power of his body accelerated dramatically when combined with the metal's strength.

He just had to wait it out.

He groaned, squeezing his eyes tight. Vaguely, he noticed the cold snow beneath him, smelled the acrid exhaust from running cars, sensed moisture on his face. But mostly, he felt searing pain throughout his right leg like he'd never felt before. He clenched his jaw tighter, trying to hold in a scream.

"Focus, dude," Bull said quietly from nearby.

Joe heard his friend praying for his healing. *Pray faster*, he wanted to say.

But he couldn't speak.

Instead, he held on tight.

CHAPTER 10

TORI sat in the passenger seat of Bull's truck as Hayley drove them to the church. The men hadn't come back inside the mall or answered their phones. The parking lot, at least the area where they'd parked that morning, looked normal. No screaming or running people, no police, but no Joe or Bull either. Tori kept telling herself not to worry. Joe had promised her that he knew what he was doing.

Hayley had reminded her a few times as well, but Tori could see she was concerned. They hadn't heard from either of the guys since that initial phone call in the food court.

That was the unspoken reason why they arrived at the church a little earlier than necessary. Just in case the guys were already there. But they weren't. And the girls were too early to meet up with everyone for the Christmas caroling party. So they busied themselves with unnecessary tasks.

They checked the bride's room to be sure there were enough chairs and tissue boxes. They peeked into the sanctuary to see if the decorating had begun. Then they walked downstairs to the fellowship hall to see if anyone had started bringing in food for tonight's rehearsal dinner.

They found a big pan covered with aluminum foil in the kitchen. They wiggled their eyebrows at each other like schoolgirls.

"Should we peek?" Tori asked. Anything to keep her mind off Joe.

"It's probably for your wedding rehearsal," Hayley said. "Or

even the wedding lunch. Nothing else requires food, right?"

Tori pulled up the edge of the aluminum foil. "Oh my gosh, I think these are Hannah's oatmeal raisin cookies," she exclaimed. "I swear, I recognize them." She inhaled deeply, the scents of cinnamon, oatmeal, and raisins making her mouth water.

Hayley giggled. "Should we have one? They must be for you."

"Split one?"

Tori waited for a nod from Hayley, and took a cookie out. It was soft and thick. She broke it in half and gave Hayley the bigger piece.

They bit into the dessert, closing their eyes in pleasure, then were startled by a man's voice.

"Gotcha!"

Tori spun toward the kitchen door and froze mid-chew. Joe's dad, Pastor Owen, walked toward them. She didn't know what else to do so she giggled, covered her mouth, finished chewing, and said, "Hello, Owen."

He grinned at them both, kissed Tori on the head, and reached for the pan. Before he lifted the foil, he looked over his shoulder toward the door. "I think she's still at the house. Have one more. I don't want to get in trouble by myself."

Hayley laughed and reached for another cookie. "I knew I liked you for a reason."

Tori hesitated. "I've got to fit into my wedding dress tomorrow, you guys."

"We walked around the mall for like," Hayley shook her head, "five hours or something. I think you've exercised enough for another cookie."

Tori grinned and took one before Owen sealed the foil around the edge again. "Hannah makes the best cookies."

"Hannah makes the best everything," Owen agreed.

"I hear my name," Hannah called from the kitchen door. She walked toward them, then stopped, hands on her hips. "Do I have to lock up all the food to keep it from being eaten?"

"Speak of an angel and she appears," Owen said.

"Don't try changing the subject, mister," Hannah scolded. She kissed him. "Just as I suspected, you taste like cinnamon and oatmeal."

Tori looked at Hayley and grinned. Owen and Hannah were so cute. She hoped that she and Joe would be like that.

"So where are the boys?" Hannah asked. "I thought they were with you today."

"They're working," said Hayley. "The mall thieves came back while we were there."

Owen and Hannah looked from Hayley to Tori and back.

"It's okay," Tori said. "Joe told me this is his job, and not to worry. I'm not worried." Okay, maybe a little, but he said to trust him, and she did.

Joe's parents look relieved, more so than Tori would have expected under the circumstances. They knew Joe worked in security. Where they always this worried about him? They looked to Hayley, who shook her head slightly.

Tori appreciated the way they all tried not to worry her or speculate about what might have happened.

"They'll probably be here anytime," Hayley said. "They know what time the caroling starts."

Both parents frowned. Hannah put her arm around Tori and pulled her toward the kitchen door. "Well then, girls, let's go get ready to sing. I hope you brought warm enough clothes."

"Aw, man!" Tori smacked her forehead. "I left my duffle with my long underwear in Joe's truck."

"Not to worry, my dear," Hannah assured her. As Hayley came up to the door from the other side of the long stainless steel table, Hannah wrapped her other arm around her shoulders, too. "This is Northern Michigan. Melissa and I have enough to go around."

By 4:45, Joe and Bull still hadn't called or shown up at the church. Tori hung back as the caroling group, including quite a few people in the wedding party, started outside.

"Go on, Tori," Owen urged her. "Sometimes in the security business things take longer than you expect."

Tori made a face. "He did say that it would be awhile if he had to file a police report."

Owen grunted in agreement. So that's where Joe got it from. "That's certainly the truth," he said.

She did want to go Christmas caroling, but she really wanted to do it with Joe.

Hayley came back inside, looking for her. "They're waiting for you."

Owen patted her back and gave her a little push. "I'm sure he'll be here by the time you're back. Have fun. Stay warm!"

Tori gave him a little wave as Hayley pulled her outside. Did Owen's expression change to worry as she stepped through the door?

It only took a few minutes for the infectious good cheer to buoy Tori's spirits. Everyone had a little book of song lyrics for the songs they would sing. Some people held fat candles, other people had flashlights. Tori decided a candle would be the most fun, and potentially warmer. She just had to remember not to get it too close to the songbook.

They walked through the neighborhood singing "Hark, the Herald Angels Sing," "Joy to the World," "Silent Night," and so many more. The darker it got, the more beautiful the scene looked with all the candles and lights. Tori was glad she'd come.

Except that Joe still hadn't arrived. She kept looking back over her shoulder, searching the darkness for him. Keeping people safe was more important than caroling, true. But he was supposed to have this week off. They'd planned for this whole day to be special, ending with their wedding rehearsal. She knew he wanted to get married, but...

Tori forced herself to ignore her doubts and believe in Joe, believe he'd be here as soon as he could. Meanwhile, she would focus on singing. That always made her feel better.

They stopped at every third or fourth house, waving to anyone who watched and waved from the windows. It was bitter cold out, and the snow that had been spitting on and off all day began to fall

in heavy fat flakes.

It was beautiful.

About twenty minutes in, as they stopped to sing in front of another house, the song leader announced that they would sing "Mary, Did You Know?" together at the marked parts, with a soloist singing the other verses. The first notes that he sang alone were rich and sweet. Tori looked around to see who was singing. He was an older black man she recognized from the choir.

As he sang, wondering aloud to Jesus' mother Mary if she knew that her baby would walk on water and give sight to a blind man, Tori felt her heart swell with the emotion of the season. There was something haunting and beautiful about the words and the tune together. Tori always felt like crying when she heard this song. With tonight's temperatures, she would have to control herself if she didn't want frostbite on her cheeks for her wedding day.

If only Joe were here. Then it would be a perfect, beautiful night.

Another twenty minutes of singing and walking, then the leader asked if people wanted to return early. Normally they would stay out for an hour or more, but most people's hats and scarves had a coating of snow on them, icy where their breath froze against the material.

Soon they were back at church. By then, even the dissenters were glad they'd returned to the warmth of the building. Hot chocolate, coffee, and cookies awaited them in the fellowship hall.

When people noticed a few of Tori and Joe's friends and relatives decorating the hall, they came over to tell her congratulations and ask where Joe was.

"He had to work," she told everyone, "he'll be here any minute."

But she was beginning to wonder. Maybe their conversation this morning had given him pause. Maybe it wasn't just that he'd gotten tied up with something. Maybe he hadn't called because he was trying to decide if he was sure now was the right time.

That seemed to be the gist of their problem. Not should they

get married — they were both convinced of their love for each other — but when. Maybe he was rethinking it and didn't know how to tell her.

Looking for ways to stay busy, Tori and Hayley helped set out paper plates and cups and plasticware for the rehearsal dinner. When Hayley took a call, Hannah called Tori into the kitchen.

"Do you think your parents will like this?" she asked, holding a fork for Tori to taste some kind of casserole.

Tori blew on it and took a bite. "Oh my *gosh*," she exclaimed. "What is that? It's amazing!"

Hannah sighed in relief. "Oh, good, I wasn't sure." She told Tori that it was an old family recipe, passed down from her grandmother on her mother's side. She explained how it was made and promised Tori she would teach her to make it, if she wanted.

"That would be wonderful, thanks, Hannah," Tori said.

Hannah looked over Tori's shoulder. "Oh, look! Joe and Bull are here. Why don't you go sit with him and we'll finish up in here."

Tori spun around. There he was, seated in the groom's chair at the front table in the hall. He looked a little tired, but he waved and smiled as he caught her eye. Tori smiled in relief and rushed over to him.

"Hey," she said as she gave him a hug, "I was beginning to wonder if you weren't coming." She'd meant it to sound teasing, but even she could hear the insecurity in her voice.

"Oh honey, I'm sorry." Joe pulled her down to sit next to him, and gave her a longer hug. "I know I should've called." He leaned back. "Check this out."

He opened his shirt pocket and pulled out several pieces of electronics that looked like they might have once been a phone. "I believe this is what is referred to as smithereens."

Tori's eyes popped open. "Holy cow! How did that happen?"

"It got run over by a car," Joe said. "Bull's phone broke, too. He tried calling Hayley several times, but it just made a bunch of weird sounds and wouldn't put the call through. But we helped catch that ring of thieves at the mall. Proud of me?"

Tori grinned and hugged him again. "Of course, I am." She looked at him more closely. "Did you get in a fight?" she asked in a quiet voice.

He shrugged one shoulder. "A little one. I'll be fine. A slight limp that will be gone by tomorrow."

Her heart gave a little stutter. How hurt was he really? Men never came clean about that kind of thing. She knew her dad and brother always tried to make injuries sound like nothing at all.

He leaned closer. "Do me a favor, wife-to-be?" He smiled at her.

Tori's heart thumped harder. All it took was his smile. Add in the loving words in that husky voice and she would do anything he asked. She nodded.

"Act like nothing's wrong, okay? I don't want to worry anyone. Do you mind? We'll sit here tonight and let them"—he nodded his head toward the roomful of guests—"come to us."

"On one condition," she said. "Promise you'll never lie to *me* about whether you're okay. I mean it. If you tell me the truth about that, I'll always trust you. And I'll back you up."

Joe raised his hand to her cheek, and gazed into her eyes. Solemnly, he said, "I'll never lie to you about whether I'm okay."

A funny picture of The Grinch crossed her mind, and her heart swelled three sizes more. Joe trusted her with his secrets. He trusted her to protect him from nosy, if well-meaning, friends. He trusted her enough to marry her. He hadn't decided to call it off.

"To prove it, I'll admit to you and you only…" He leaned over and whispered into her ear, *"Ow."* He chuckled a little. "I'd like to give what-for to the guy who hit me, I'll tell you what. But I controlled myself."

"Tell me where it hurts so I don't touch you there," Tori said. "Then tell me where to find the guy and I'll beat him up for you."

Joe laughed and hugged her. "Want to know a little secret?" he asked. He pulled her chair closer, and spoke low in her ear. "I asked Bull not to tell anyone, but I wanted to share it with you. In fact, I wished you were there."

He told her about a boy he'd met recently, how he had an opportunity to buy stolen food for his family for Christmas, and how Joe had promised to bring Christmas dinner for them as a reward, of sorts, for the boy doing the right thing.

Tori felt tears near the surface. *Wonderful* and *amazing* weren't adequate descriptors of this man. How did she get so lucky?

"It was hard to explain that I wanted to do this to help him, but that he wouldn't always be rewarded for doing the right thing. Sometimes, in fact, it seems like you get punished for making the right choice."

Tori nodded. "That's a hard lesson. Hopefully, you made it a little easier for him to learn."

"Bull was there, helping me deliver the food, and he's great with kids. He did a better job of encouraging Jackson and his little brothers and sister than I ever would've. I'm glad he was there."

Tori and Joe talked quietly for a few minutes, catching up on their time apart. Tori told him about sneaking cookies with Hayley and Owen. Joe wished he'd been there for that. And he wasn't surprised the carolers came back early. It wasn't fun weather to drive in, let alone walk in.

Soon, the dinner started. Joe limped as they headed to the food tables, but Tori walked slowly, saying hi to people, so no one would notice his limp. Both sets of parents gave heartfelt toasts, making Tori cry both times.

Everyone ate and talked and laughed until Owen finally called them upstairs to rehearse in the sanctuary. Joe and Tori grabbed two more oatmeal cookies, giggling together like children. Then Hayley and Bull joined them, and the few cookies left, vanished.

"Hey, let's take the elevator," Bull said, "so no one sees us eating the rest of the cookies."

Tori squeezed his arm and smiled at him. She'd been trying to think of a way to get Joe on the elevator without undermining his manliness. Bull patted her hand and winked.

Partway through the rehearsal, which would've gone much faster if there was less horseplay, one of Joe's brothers came in and

announced that the snow was getting worse.

Most everyone went to the windows and doors to look out. Owen spoke quietly to his other son, then Hannah joined them. Danny walked over, followed closely by Dixie.

"You get the feeling they're planning our demise?" Joe asked.

He started to get up and Bull put a hand on his shoulder. "Down boy," he said, "let that leg heal for tomorrow."

It sure looked like Joe had nailed it. Tori saw both mothers look over at her and Joe a time or two. It didn't look good.

Owen walked back to the front of the church. "Can everyone come up here, please?" He waited for people to get close enough to hear him.

"Eddie has an updated weather report and it's not good. We're supposed to get at least a foot of snow tonight, and it may not stop there. I know most of you are pretty local, but bad weather can be nerve-wracking whether you're driving for an hour or a few blocks."

Owen looked at Tori and Joe, and Tori knew what was coming next. The way Joe squeezed her hand, he did, too.

"We think you should consider postponing long enough for the weather to clear. For safety's sake."

Tori wanted to shout at them all for trying once again to stop their wedding. But who was she going to blame this time — God? She sighed and looked at Joe. She wouldn't cry. But she wasn't going to roll over and let other people dictate her life. She and Joe would decide their fate.

He put his arm around her and pulled her tight against him. Hayley took Tori's free hand and squeezed it. Bull leaned in close from Joe's other side. Tori felt like a fortress of friendship surrounded and supported her. Despite the situation, it almost made her smile.

"What do you think?" Joe asked her quietly so no one but the four of them could hear.

She studied his expression. They hadn't had time to finish their conversation this morning, but both of them were here. Neither one of them had backed out when the excuses were vague warnings about the future. She didn't think either of them wanted to back

out now, even with this clear and compelling reason to postpone.

"I think," she said slowly, "that we need a minister and two witnesses." She looked around the room. "Which we have."

Joe's eyes widened a bit when he caught her meaning. "Do it now?"

"It would be a shame for so many people to miss it if the weather clears," Hayley said. "Mickey's not here."

"We don't have any of our wedding clothes," Bull said. "But we don't live far. We could run and get them. Still, if we were to go out in the weather now, why not go out in the morning? Even if it ends up being just the four of us."

Despite the fighting over the wedding, Tori still wanted all of her family there. She only planned to do it once.

"What about the people who might get snowed in tonight?" Hayley asked.

Bull shrugged. "I'm an early riser." He looked over his shoulder at the waiting sets of parents and turned back to Joe. "Give me addresses of who you absolutely want to be here tomorrow, and I'll call some of our friends. We'll dig everyone out in the morning in time to get here by eleven." He looked at Hayley and said, "We can split up a list of the guests and start making calls letting them know the wedding is still on, but only to come out if they feel comfortable driving in the weather."

Hayley smiled at Bull, then said to Tori, "We'll be sure everyone knows you guys understand if they don't want to drive. We'll remind your relatives of the reception your moms are throwing when you get back from your honeymoon."

Tori looked at Joe and smiled. The generosity of their friends amazed her. "Well?"

Joe kissed her soundly. "Looks like we're still going to have our Christmas Eve wedding."

CHAPTER 11

JOE woke up slowly. Such weird dreams last night. In the one he remembered best, he was helping Iron Man save New York from aliens. One alien attacked him from behind and Joe went down. He woke up in Tony Stark's lab, connected by wires to the inside of the Iron Man suit, healing faster than ever.

That was a fun dream. Joe wished he didn't have to wake up. He felt Snickers move beside him, and he reached over to scratch his cat.

"Hey, buddy. What day is it anyhow? I feel wrecked."

Snickers purred and stretched under his hand.

Joe rolled onto his back and felt something hard. He reached behind him and retrieved an iron pipe. As the metal touched his hand, a gentle whoosh of energy rippled through his body. All the memories of the day before rushed to the surface.

Today was his wedding day!

Joe sat up and pulled back the covers, much to Snickers' annoyance. All kinds of metalworks were taped to most of his body. Only a couple of pieces had come off in the night. He checked out his right thigh.

Last night, Bull had helped him into his dad's office while Tori and his mom were out with the carolers. They made sure no one saw them because he could hardly walk. Owen had acted like a father first, then a field medic, then the Guild leader — he'd hugged his son, then made Joe undress to his boxers so he could examine his wounds, then reprimanded him for getting in a fight

without his super suit.

"That's why Mickey put the body armor in it!" he yelled.

That's when Joe knew his leg was as damaged as it felt. "Pastor" Owen rarely yelled.

His dad and Bull had argued with him about going to the hospital. Joe reminded them that every time he'd gone in the past, his body was mostly healed by the time he ever got to see a doctor.

So they decided to tape as much iron and steel to his body as they could, and see how he felt at the end of the wedding rehearsal. Bull and Owen raided Owen's garage and came back with an impressive collection of wrenches and pipes, and a roll of duct tape.

Joe saw the tape and demanded Bull get a roll of paper towels. The metal needed to be in contact with his skin for him to gain power from it, but he wanted a layer of paper towels before they taped everything down.

"I don't want to explain to my wife on our honeymoon why it looks like I wax my legs," he said.

"Plus it would hurt like Hades," Bull chuckled.

Last night, when Joe had seen his leg for the first time — and that was after two hours of healing — his entire right hip and thigh was a huge black bruise.

Looking at it this morning, Joe was amazed to see much of the bruising had already faded to yellow. Still sitting on the bed, he flexed his knee, bringing his heel to his buttocks, listening for any crunching sounds. He hadn't wanted to admit it to his dad, but Joe felt pretty confident he'd broken a bone.

The flexing didn't hurt, so Joe did it again. Still no crunching noise.

"Thank you, God," he breathed. He sagged with relief, letting his face fall into his hands. His wedding day could have gone very differently, very *badly*.

He moved Snickers and swung his legs over the side of his bed. No vertigo or nausea. No pain in his leg, hip, knee, back. He was about ready to stand up when something caught his attention. He sniffed the air.

Bacon.

Joe stood, giving himself another minute to test his leg. Everything seemed to work fine. It didn't hurt, just felt like he'd knocked his leg against something.

Yeah, something like *a lug wrench.*

The door opened and his little brother, Stuart, walked in. "Hey, morning, I'm supposed to — aw, for Pete's sake, put some shorts on, will ya? I'm supposed to check your leg, see if we need to leave the hardware taped on or not. Then feed you all the protein and vitamin C you can inhale."

As he spoke, Stuart waited for Joe to pull his boxers on, then he checked out Joe's leg, prodding it and looking at the bruises on the back that Joe couldn't see.

"How's it look?" Joe asked, trying to twist around.

Stuart stood up. "You scared the hell out of us last night, man." He gave Joe a hard backslapping hug. "I can't believe how much better it looks. Can you walk on it?"

Joe cocked an eyebrow at him. "I walked on it last night." He moved to the closet, to the bathroom door, to the dresser, and back without limping.

Stuart snorted. "I mean, does it hurt?"

Joe grinned. "Wanna dance?"

"You're such a blockhead. Why would you get in a fight without—"

Joe held up his hand. "Save it. I heard it from Mom and Dad last night, and Mickey before that. I'm sure I'll hear more today. When's that bacon gonna be ready?"

"Shoot!" Stuart shot out the door and took the steps two at a time. A moment later, he shouted, "Saved! Come and get it."

Joe chuckled and pulled on some sweats. He picked up Snickers and started gingerly down the stairs. Nothing hurt, nothing creaked, nothing acted any differently.

Except that he still had every wrench his dad owned taped to his legs and arms. That felt pretty weird.

Downstairs, Stuart put a mound of scrambled eggs covered in

another mound of bacon in front of him. Joe raised his eyebrows at his brother and chuckled in disbelief.

"Mom said." Stuart planted two tall glasses of orange juice in front of him. "By the way, you're out of eggs now." He brought another plate of bacon and eggs to the kitchen table for himself. "Thank you, God, for keeping Dopey here from getting killed, and please bless him and Tori with an awesome day."

Joe grinned. "Amen." They both dug into their breakfasts. Joe was pleasantly surprised. "Since when can you cook?"

Stuart chewed and swallowed. "Since I'm in college and don't eat at normal times." He ate a huge forkful of eggs. "Mom's been bribing me. She's only been teaching me how to make my favorite foods. So far, I can do bacon and eggs, hamburgers and frozen French fries, and chocolate chip cookies."

"A balanced diet." Joe heard a sound from the front of the house and turned. "Was that a snowplow?"

"Bull dug out your truck already. It's still snowing, but pretty lightly. If that was a plow, I'll go shovel out what the plow threw in the drive after you get out of the shower."

Joe gave his brother a questioning look.

Stuart rolled his eyes. "Mom said to talk to you while you shower so I can help you if you pass out or fall or something."

The two of them looked at each other for a moment, then burst out laughing.

"Yeah, yeah, well, she was wiping at her eyes and pretending she wasn't crying, so I'm going to do as she asked. We can talk about my list of souvenirs I want you to look for at Disney World."

After breakfast, Stuart cut all the duct tape off Joe and lay the metal tools aside. Joe sat on his bed in his boxers again, trying to decide how he felt. Definitely weaker.

"So now I know for sure where my strength comes from," he said.

"Psalm 121, man," said his brother. "Anyone else would be laid up for weeks. You wanna lie down?"

Joe shook his head. He did, but it was already 8:30 a.m. "I

want to get to the church."

Stuart chuckled. "I guess it's a good sign for your marriage that you're an eager groom."

Joe showered without incident, so Stuart went to clear the end of the driveway while Joe shaved. As he ran the blade down his cheeks, he thought about Tori's reactions last night. He'd asked his friends and family to keep her occupied until he could sit down so she wouldn't see him stumble in.

He rinsed the blade under the water and glanced at his bruised leg. He'd been badly hurt yesterday. It was stupid to keep going like he did. And the way Tori treated the situation calmly, helping him without making it noticeable, he was more convinced than ever that they were going to make a great team.

Joe promised himself now that if he ever got hurt like that again, he'd allow himself to be taken to the hospital. Testing his limits was hardly worth finding out the hard way what his body couldn't heal by itself.

His home phone rang. He glanced up in surprise. He rarely got calls on his home number. Then he remembered that his cell phone looked worse than he did. He walked over and answered the extension by his bed.

"Hey, Joe." Detective Arturo Paredes of the SLU was on the other end. His voice came through with a cheerful ring. "I wanted to give you a little Christmas gift. Those guys you and your team caught for us at the mall yesterday, confirmation just came in that we got them all. Thanks to your friend, Tick Tock, we were able to find the vans the thieves were filling, *and* the warehouse they used to store and sell the merchandise."

"That's great news, Art," Joe said, a sense of pride and accomplishment washing over him. "Thanks for letting me know."

"I heard you got hurt helping us take them down, and I wanted you to know it was worth it. We found guns in two of the cars. We think they might've been looking to upgrade their efforts."

"Wow." Joe hated to think what would've happened to the young woman in the Mercedes who fought the thieves for her

packages. And he definitely didn't want to think of what would've happened if his attacker had used a gun instead of a lug wrench.

"Yeah," Art said, "bad news. But the good news is they're off the street, thanks to you. Listen, I know you're getting married today — congratulations — so I'll let you get back to it. Merry Christmas!"

"Merry Christmas, Art," Joe said. "Thanks for the call."

When he clicked off, he stared at his phone for a moment. Then he smiled into the mirror. He had a hard job, but he made a difference in people's lives. That was worth it.

He finished shaving, dressed in his tuxedo sans bow tie, and patted on some cologne. If his wet hair didn't freeze into icicles between here and church, he was about ready.

Stuart helped him load his suitcase and duffle into the truck, then Joe put Snickers in his carrier and grabbed the bag of cat stuff Stuart and Melissa would need for the week.

"Got everything?" Stuart asked from the door.

"Just need me a bride," Joe said with a grin, and locked up his house.

At the church, the parking lot was plowed and there were a lot of cars already there. Inside, there were *a lot* more people, most walking around with cups of coffee and baked goods.

Joe turned to Stuart and found his brother grinning widely.

"Bull and Mickey and your other friends starting picking people up an hour ago and bringing them in, then going out for more. Mom's Bible study came in to make coffee and muffins for everyone while they waited. And three deacons came over to plow the parking lot and shovel the sidewalks. I think they're shoveling them a second time already."

Joe stood there with his mouth open, stunned.

"After you two leave for the airport, we'll start ferrying everyone back to their homes," Stuart said. "I wanted to hang with you this morning, so I'm on duty later."

"When did everyone decide to do all this?" Joe asked. "I just saw all you guys last night."

Stuart shrugged. "You know how it is at church, kind of an avalanche effect." He swung his head toward the weather outside. "No pun intended."

Joe was still feeling a little punch-drunk when his mother came around the corner. "There you are!" She hugged him tight, then kissed his cheek. "How's my boy?" she asked in a quieter voice.

"I'm fine, Mom," he said, returning her hug.

"Stuart, how is he?" she asked.

"He's in better shape than I was when he tackled me playing touch football at Thanksgiving," he said. "And he ate everything you wanted him to, washed behind his ears, and packed his teddy bear for his honeymoon."

Hannah pressed her lips together and smacked her youngest son in the shoulder. Then she hugged him, too. "Thank you for being there," she said, her feelings running close to the surface, making her voice quiver.

"I'm glad he came over," Joe said. "We watched old movies and braided each other's hair."

Both men laughed when Hannah smacked Joe's shoulder, too.

"Come with me." She took Joe's hand. "Let's go see your father. Stuart, get something to eat."

Hannah led Joe to his dad's office. He could guess what they wanted to discuss with him, but at least with the obvious wedding activity going on, canceling the wedding was finally off the list of potential topics. He figured it would be about seeing a doctor or telling Tori about the family's legacy of powers.

"Joe, how are you?" Owen got up from his desk and hugged his son hard, then slapped him on the back. He pulled back only enough to leave his hands on Joe's shoulders. "How's the leg?"

Bingo. First guess. "It's good," Joe said. "The bruises are already yellow, and I'm not limping. No pain."

"Let's see," said his mother. Joe walked to the door and back. "No, let's see your leg," she insisted.

"Mom, I'm twenty-nine years old. I'm not taking my pants off in front of you. It's fine. If you don't believe me, ask Stuart." Joe

loved his parents, but they never seemed to stop…parenting.

"Your mother wants you to get an x-ray," Owen said, hands on his hips.

Hannah cleared her throat.

"We both do," his dad amended.

Joe took a deep breath. He normally believed in the wisdom of "pick your battles." But there was quite literally no time to get an x-ray, get married, and get on a plane by three o'clock today.

It was possible his dad would let up on his "tell Tori" campaign if Joe gave in on this item. But then they'd be a day or two late for their honeymoon. He'd rather be relaxing with Tori than hanging out with his family, wishing he were alone with his new wife.

He thought of where in particular he'd like to be relaxing with her. Hey, right. Bed rest.

"If there were time, I would do it just to set your minds at ease," he said. "But without saying too much to my *parents*"—he eyed them both sternly—"I'm going to spend much of the next week in bed. If the leg starts hurting again, I'll get an x-ray right away. I promise."

His mom and dad looked at each other and did that silent communication thing they did. He wondered when he and Tori would start doing that. No doubt it would irritate their children. That would be fun.

"All right," Owen finally said. "We're trusting you on this. But as Guild leader, I'm giving you a verbal warning about getting involved in hand-to-hand combat without proper equipment."

Joe opened his mouth to object. A verbal warning would be passed on to his team leader, Mickey. Written warnings about a Paladin could affect his whole team, keeping them from coveted assignments. A verbal warning, on the other hand, wouldn't be a mark against Joe in the same way, but he'd never done anything to warrant anything but praise from his father in the past. This seemed unfair.

And yet, there was the "pick your battles" bit of wisdom. The warning wouldn't hurt him as he worked his way up the ranks. He

just needed to nod and take it.

Nod and take it. He gritted his teeth.

Then he nodded. "Okay."

Owen gave a slight nod, then lowered his eyes. Joe wondered if his dad didn't want to give the warning. He could have easily let it go. But good leaders couldn't let things slide, not even with — especially not with — their own family. Joe suspected this was a lesson he needed to learn as he worked his way into his father's position. He gave his father a nod of respect.

"So what's the update on Tori and her family?" Owen asked. "What do they know?"

Joe turned his face away for a moment, working on controlling his temper. Just hit all the soft spots at once, Dad. Geez. And on his wedding day.

"Dad, no matter what Tori knows or when, nothing is going to change with her family," he said firmly. "I *literally* saved her dad's life on Saturday, and they still refuse to believe superheroes are real. We're going to have to keep everyone from letting their powers show when her family is around. I'm sorry, but I don't know what more I can do."

Owen rubbed the back of his neck. Hannah sighed and folded her arms.

"Honey, we can't make them believe," she said gently.

"I know, but…" Owen shook his head. "Joe, I've counseled hundreds of people over the years who are head over heels in love, but have some difficult hurdles they'll have to jump to make their marriages last. A secret like this is going to make every part of your marriage harder. Every. Part."

"It's going to be fine, Dad." Joe said the words as sincerely as he could mange considering he wasn't sure he believed them himself.

But what more could he say? He didn't want to share his private conversations with his fiancée, but maybe it would help to tell his parents a little.

"We've talked about secrets, about finding out unexpected

things about each other over time. She was wonderful last night, didn't freak out, didn't even let on she knew I was hurt."

"You told her?" Hannah asked.

"Yeah, I told her almost everything, and she took it like a pro." Joe felt himself feeling proud of her. She was going to make a great wife, period, but eventually she would be a fantastic Paladin's wife.

"Well, that's good, right?" Hannah asked his dad.

Owen shuffled his feet around and stared at the ceiling for a moment. "I just don't know. I don't know if I should marry you, knowing what I do."

"Dad…" Joe tried to hide his frustration. "This is my wedding day."

"It's not you, son," Owen said, but he couldn't meet Joe's eyes. "This is about me, about *my* integrity."

Joe sighed deeply. There was no argument for that. After a moment he said, "So I tell her, try to make her understand something she's been led her whole life to believe is a lie, try to explain that I'm not nuts, *the hour before we're to get married*, and hope she still marries me, or you might decide in the next hour not to go through with this."

Owen didn't say anything, just stared at his shoes.

"Be fair, Joe," his mom said quietly. "Your father has been asking this of you since the day you got engaged. The timing here is on you, son."

Joe stared hard at her for a moment, arranging his argument in his head. Then he dropped his eyes, turned, and walked out of the room.

His mom was right.

TORI stood in front of the full-length mirror in the bride's room at church. She smoothed down the folds of her wedding dress as Lexie zipped and buttoned. Hayley stood by the edge of the mirror

putting on her makeup. Dixie stood to the side, directing.

Tori smiled at herself in the mirror.

Look at you. *A bride.* She almost couldn't believe it.

And she looked so beautiful. Hayley had done her hair, swept up on the top of her head with lovely little curls trailing down. Her mother had added sprigs of real holly and baby's breath as she attached the veil.

Joe had given her a pair of pale blue sapphire earrings last night before they left the church. They sparkled in the light when she moved her head. She loved them. She loved that Joe gave them to her and didn't care if they were paste or real. But the way they sparkled, she wondered.

This morning, her mother had surprised her by opening a very old velvet jewelry box and pulling out a dainty chain with a single pearl. As she attached the clasp around Tori's neck, she said, "My father gave this to my mother when they got married. It was her 'something new.' Then she gave it to me when I married"—she cleared her throat—"your father. My 'something old.'"

She stood back and adjusted the pearl against Tori's throat. "Now I'm giving it to you as your 'something old.' I'd love it if you loaned it to your sisters when they get married as their 'something borrowed.'" She smiled at Lexie. "If they'd like that."

Tori hugged her mom tight. She didn't want to let go. When she sniffled, Lexie and Hayley jumped in with tissues and washcloths dipped in cold water. The cloths were pressed against her face to keep her eyes from getting red and puffy. Tori laughed at the commotion and blew her nose.

"*This,*" Hayley said, "is why I said I'd do everyone's makeup at the last minute. Come on, Lex, get in here and get the crying over with."

Lexie pulled something from her pocket. Tori recognized it immediately.

"Your dress is 'something new' so I wanted to loan you my count-your-blessings bracelet for 'something borrowed.' It's one of my most treasured possessions."

Tori tried to saw, "Aw, thank you," but it came out as "Aw, sob, sob."

She remembered the day she bought it. Lexie's boyfriend-about-to-be-fiancé had declared he wasn't interested in being a father and had left the week before. Lexie was close to inconsolable.

Tori was at Target, the most expensive store she could afford, buying toilet paper and dish soap and wondering how to make her sister feel better. She walked by the jewelry counter and saw this pretty little charm bracelet for twenty dollars. The thought popped into her head that this could be a way for Lexie to count her blessings, focus on the positive things in her life — which seemed few and far between the last few years.

A few charms lay on a small tray. Two caught her eye — one of two little girls holding hands, one of a baby carriage. They were ten dollars each. Tori stood staring at them, unable to shake the feeling that this simple gift might bring Lexie back from the brink.

Though she hated to ask her parents for help, she didn't have enough money for the gift *and* the toilet paper and soap. She put the other things back, told herself it would be better to let go of her pride if it might help her sister, and bought the jewelry.

Lexie had loved the gift. She heard Tori's unspoken warning that she could lose herself in grief like she had as a teenager, and she forced herself to let go of her heartache and focus on the blessing of her unborn baby. And, Lexie had told her, the blessing of her sister.

With that memory between them, Tori and Lexie held on to each other for a long minute. Tori cried and Lexie tried to keep it in, as was her habit.

Then Lexie fastened the bracelet on Tori's right wrist, and said, "We've both got more blessings than this bracelet can hold, but I'm glad you're getting another one."

Her sister couldn't have said anything more eloquent. For all that they'd tried to protect each other from the havoc and heartache in the world, Lexie wasn't upset that Tori had found love. Tori felt a few more tears slip out as she hugged her sister again. When she pulled back, she saw Hayley and her mom wiping their eyes, too.

"Okay, are we done now?" Hayley asked. "I've got to do our makeup soon."

Tori laughed and wiped the cool cloth across her face. "Done." Hayley was as good as Lexie at hiding her emotions. But an entire day of emotional displays was about going to kill them.

Standing in front of the mirror now, Tori could see all three of them fussing over her, trying to help make her day perfect. She felt a sudden sense of peace wash over her. Not just a feeling of being "okay." But a supernatural strength of purpose that permeated every cell.

It was a feeling she always associated with God's presence. She took a deep breath and smiled into the mirror. She knew the tears were behind her now, even the happy ones. The strength and peace in her heart were a sign that life was going exactly as it should.

Just like the rhyme, she now had something old and something new, something borrowed and something blue. If there was a "something holy" brides should have on their wedding day, it was this peace.

A knock sounded at the door. Her mom went to answer it.

"Must be a man," Lexie said as she put finishing touches to Tori's lip gloss.

All the women could come and go as they pleased, but no men were allowed in the bride's room. Mostly because all the women dressed in there together, although Tori figured the original idea was to preserve the sense of mystery and surprise.

"Joe, you can't see her now," Tori heard her mom saying.

"What does he need?" Tori asked.

"I just need a minute," Joe called from the hallway.

"Be right back," she told the girls.

"Tori, he can't see you before the wedding," they complained.

As Tori approached the door, Dixie closed it to a crack and said, "Here she comes. Turn your back, at least."

Tori waved her mother away and Dixie left reluctantly, shaking her head. Tori stood hidden behind the door and spoke into the crack. "Hey, Joe," she said, keeping her voice quiet enough for his

ears only. "How are you?"

Joe sighed. "It's good to hear your voice."

He didn't say anything more. Tori closed her eyes and breathed in the scent of him. "You're wearing my favorite cologne."

"I bet you'll think I look as good as I smell."

Tori could hear the smile in his voice. "I can't wait to see you," she said softly. "But I always think you look good."

They were both quiet for a moment. "You okay?" she asked.

There was a long pause. "Do you want to know all my secrets? Right now? I'll tell you every detail about me right now so you can be sure you want to marry me."

Tori heard the almost desperate worry in his voice. She looked over at the clock on the wall. Ten minutes to eleven. She closed her eyes and felt that enormous blanket of peace inside.

Please, God, help Joe feel your peace.

"Joe?" she said softly. "Are you listening to me?"

"Yes."

"I am so sure I want to marry you, I'm willing to learn all your secrets over the next sixty years. That's the way everyone else does it. But if you absolutely have to tell me something, you can tell me tonight, in our hotel room, in bed." She couldn't believe she'd just said that! She felt a grin stretch her lips. As much as she looked forward to consummating their marriage, she'd never spoken about it out loud. "I'll listen to whatever you want to say then. Okay?"

After a pause, Joe chuckled softly. "It's a deal, almost-wife."

"All right then," she said. "Isn't there somewhere you need to be, almost-husband?"

"Yes, ma'am," he said. "I'll see you in a few minutes."

Tori felt a huge grin on her face as she shut the door. She leaned there for a moment thinking, *he's almost my husband! I'm almost his wife!*

The women finished their final preparations, then Tori's dad came to escort her mom to the front of the church.

Dixie gently pulled the long gossamer-thin veil over Tori's face. "You're a most beautiful bride," she said.

Tori smiled widely. "Thank you."

A minute later, there was another knock on the door. "Everyone decent?" Owen called.

"Come in," she said. "Are you ready for us?" She was so excited now that the moment was upon her, she almost couldn't contain herself.

"Bridesmaids and flower girls to the front," Owen confirmed. "I'll chat with the bride for a moment."

Hayley and Lexie blew kisses to her and left. Tori felt her smile widen as she turned back to Joe's dad.

"I'm so excited," she said. "My stomach is doing a little dance."

Owen chuckled with her. Then he asked, "Joe came to talk to you?"

She nodded. "Yes, poor nervous man."

Owen looked around the empty room. "And he told you… his secret?"

There were moments when Tori equally loved both sets of parents, and also wanted to move far away from them. They all wanted to be just a little too involved.

But the strength of the peace she felt muted her frustrations. She wanted to be generous and loving with them, especially on her wedding day. She took his hand in hers. "We are going to be fine, Owen. Joe and I are going to get through this together."

Owen half-nodded and half shook his head. "This… meaning…?"

He was making her nervous. Her stomach twitched. Whatever Joe wanted to tell her, he could tell her tonight. Alone. With all the weeks of people trying to stop the wedding, she just wanted to get on with it before her stomach took flight on its own. She smiled up at him and squeezed his hand.

"We are going to be fine. You don't have to worry about us." It felt like the energy building in her abdomen escaped with her words. She felt better.

Owen tilted his head at her, frowning. Then he smiled faintly back. "You're going to be fine. I won't worry about you two."

His words sounded stilted, but Tori smiled and squeezed his hand again. "Good. Here's my dad. Are we ready?"

Owen nodded, looking a little strange with a half-smile, half-frown. Danny led Tori down to the doors at the entrance to the sanctuary while Owen went a back way to come out in front next to Joe and the groomsmen.

Tori heard singing inside the sanctuary. It was beautiful, haunting, and full of emotion. "Who's that?" she asked her dad.

"Joe's friend, Mickey," he said. "Amazing voice, huh?"

The song ended. At the brief silence, Tori knew the pianist had moved to the organ. She smiled up at her dad.

"My little girl is getting married," he said, a catch in his voice. "You look like sunshine." He looked down at her and Tori felt enveloped in over two decades of his love.

"I don't deserve you, Daddy," she said, "but I'm glad I have you."

He started to say something, then cleared his throat and wiped at his eyes. He faced forward, patting and rubbing her hand on his arm.

Tori smiled and faced forward. This amazing joyful peace filled her in such a way that she didn't feel the usual push of tears that strong emotions always brought out. She was such a heart-on-her-sleeve kind of girl. But today she felt stronger and more confident than she'd ever felt in her life.

As the organ music played, Bull led Lexie down the aisle, little Ben the ring-bearer walking in front of them. Then Joe's oldest brother Carl walked Hayley down the aisle. Two of Joe's younger nieces followed throwing out flower petals.

And then it was her turn.

Danny led her to the door. The crowd stood. A much bigger crowd than she expected on this snowy December day. At the front, Owen nodded to the man standing next to him.

Joe turned around.

Her Joe.

She smiled at him, feeling like she was indeed a sun burning

brightly just for him.

The music played and Danny led her forward. When he put her hand in Joe's, Tori felt like she was going to burst, her body hardly able to contain all the joy she felt.

She tried to focus on every detail of the service, to memorize it all, to enjoy every moment. But she felt like they moved on a helium cloud, a beautiful gravity-free dance that culminated in the words —

"I now pronounce you husband and wife."

Tori barely registered that Joe's dad sounded happy. She watched as Joe lifted her veil over her head, his hands shaking. She leaned forward.

He cupped her face in his hands and kissed her tenderly, sweetly. She raised her face to enjoy all the promises in that kiss, one hand lifted to cover his, the blessings bracelet tinkling near her ear.

Joe pulled back a little and they grinned at each other. He leaned his forehead against hers and whispered, "We did it."

The joy inside tumbled out in Tori's laughter. Then Joe leaned back his head and gave a loud, "Whoop!"

Their friends and family burst into laughing applause.

Joe wrapped his arms around her, and kissed her with passion and abandon, leaning her back over his arm. Tori kissed him until she thought she was going to lose her balance. She began to laugh.

He pulled her up tight to his chest, put one hand on her cheek again, and said, "I'm never gonna let you go."

The next hour was a whirlwind of hugs and congratulations, a quick parade of pictures with the photographer — in attendance only because Bull had driven across the city to pick him up — and a fairly quick, light lunch that Tori could barely eat.

Joe rarely let go of her hand, and she couldn't stop grinning at him.

Soon, her bridesmaids were helping her change into her going-away dress. Hannah and Dixie pressed a bag of wrapped sandwiches and other snacks into Joe's hand for the plane ride. Hugs and kisses

and not a few tears later, the two of them pulled on their coats and ran to Joe's truck.

Someone had already started the engine and turned on the heat. Bless them.

Joe pulled Tori close and fastened the middle seat belt around her waist. "I don't want you too far away," he said.

Tori grinned up at him with a mile-wide smile. "I'm not going anywhere."

He rolled down the windows so they could wave at everyone willing to brave the cold. Then he put the truck in gear. "You ready to start our new adventure together?"

"Yes!" Tori laughed.

Nothing could make her happier.

TWO things always surprised Joe Clarke at Christmas: the weather and the people of Double Bay.

Barely a week ago, there had been no snow to add a Christmas-y touch to the festive season. Today, without the help of friends and family, that freshly fallen snow would have kept him from getting married.

Ah, yes, the wonderful citizens of Double Bay constantly surprised him. They organized calling parties to let the wedding guests know that the wedding was still on. They organized driving parties to pick up those too afraid to brave the snow-covered streets. They even organized a baking party to feed the guests as they arrived at the celebration hours early.

As Joe drove to the airport with his bride, he counted his blessings, overwhelmed with the avalanche that had been tumbling down around them for days. He turned on the radio to the station that played all Christmas music this time of year. One of his favorite bands, Pentatonix, was singing.

Hark the herald angels sing, glory to the newborn King!

A Double Bay police car pulled up next to Joe and flashed its lights. Detective Arturo Paredes of the Superhero Liaison Unit waved and grinned and pulled ahead.

A police escort. Joe grinned. Time to hightail it out of town with his girl.

CHAPTER 1

TORI Lewis was out of M&M'S. None in her purse, none in the glove box. Even the emergency packet in her briefcase had been consumed during her pre-wedding jitters. After the job interview she'd just endured for Half TV, a local cable TV station, she needed a chocolate fix. Now.

"I know I'm supposed to go to you for comfort," she muttered to God as she pulled into a parking spot, "but if you wouldn't mind, a package of M&M'S would jumpstart the process."

The bell tinkled over her head as the door of Ed & Eddie's Corner Market closed behind her. Tori stamped the snow off her boots as her eyes adjusted from the deepening twilight outside to the bright fluorescent lights of the store. It took her a moment to notice everyone in the store staring at her. Including the guy with the gun.

Tori froze. She always assumed her love of the colorful chocolate candy might one day destroy her figure, but she never expected her addiction to end in gunfire.

The gunman swung toward her. His bulky open coat couldn't hide the fact that the skinny boy was no man. A Detroit Tigers baseball cap covered most of his brown hair, but not his panicky eyes. "What do you want?" His voice came out higher at the end and he cleared his throat. "Well?" he asked, forcing the word out at a lower pitch.

"Uhh…M&M'S," Tori said. It sounded like a question. Her brain was having a hard time getting up to speed in this unexpected situation. *God, help me.*

Her eyes darted around the small store. An older woman

cried and held a nearly hysterical younger woman, shushing her to no avail. One of the men held a baby ensconced in a little pink snowsuit. Another nodded quietly at her as if to convey caution.

Situation confirmed. She was hip-deep in doo-doo. Where was her big, strong new husband when she needed him?

The armed boy-man cocked his head toward the candy aisle. Tori didn't know if he meant for her to move out of the way or if he was just being unusually helpful by pointing her in the right direction. Erring on the side of caution, she forced a fleeting smile and mumbled "thanks" as she walked past him and down the middle aisle to stand in front of the M&M'S. Now what?

The gunman turned back to Eddie, the cashier and half-owner of Ed & Eddie's. "Hurry up before someone else comes in!"

"Easy, dude, easy," Eddie said, moving his hands slowly toward the cash register. Eddie wasn't very old either, early 20s or so, but he was sadly experienced in the holdup category. Tori couldn't remember the details, but she'd heard bits and pieces of stories. Come to think of it, why did she shop at a store with a record anyway? She remembered Eddie had played sports in high school. Something like baseball or wrestling or karate could come in handy right now. Hopefully his sport hadn't been cross-country running.

Tori glanced at the M&M'S next to her. More than ever she needed to stress eat. Could she open a package now and pay Eddie later? Maybe two packages. Her hands started to shake. She shoved them in her pockets.

Today was only day ten of her new and fabulous married life. She hadn't wanted to go out today anyway and now this. Only two days ago she and Joe had checked out of their Disney World hotel, blue skies and temperatures in the 70s, nothing on their minds but a long and blissful life together. Tori prayed now that she'd make it to day eleven of that life. They hadn't been married long enough to do anything except have sex — which was *awesome* — but she'd hoped for more. After all, they figured they'd have the rest of their lives together. Neither of them thought the "death" part of "till death do us part" would happen until there was a lot more gray

hair involved.

The sound of a crying baby registered. Tori glanced over at the well-dressed man in the expensive trench coat. He kept his back between the gunman and his child. A gesture Tori would normally find heartwarming. But today it was the action of a man who wasn't going to get involved. Great. He wouldn't be of any use. So this is where equal opportunity gets us. Tori considered offering to hold the baby so he could help the other men save the day. Her self-esteem would be fine with that. Maybe if she were comforting someone, she wouldn't feel like crying herself.

Enough! Tori wiped at her eyes. She was not letting some stupid, scared boy dictate her life and death. She'd spent too much energy changing her life into just what she wanted to lose it now. She chewed on her lip. What could she do?

A movement from the corner of her eye. She saw one of the men — the one who'd nodded calmly at her — edging closer to the gunman. Yikes. Should she duck or help?

A POLICE car raced past the entrance to Harborview Mall. Lights and sirens cleared a path among the post-Christmas shoppers. But mostly people moved to avoid the speeding white Toyota hurtling through the night like a rusty snowball.

The cars sped through two more lights. Divine intervention surely prevented a crash as the Toyota skidded on a patch of ice, nearly sideswiping another car. The police cruiser missed that particular bit of ice, but a close call at the next light had the cop in the passenger seat crossing himself with one hand while hanging on with the other.

Another police car parked in the next intersection forced the chase to take a hard right and brought them into a quieter industrial area. Quieter except for the jarring sirens. Large warehouse-style office buildings magnified the piercing sound and reflected the

red and blue lights onto the snow. The Toyota picked up speed, blowing through three stop signs amidst honking horns and flying middle fingers.

The police cars slowed down enough to ensure that the chase continued to be accident-free. The Toyota made a left down an alley to avoid yet another police car, and raced out of sight.

SUPERHERO X looked up at the roof of the nearby three-story office building and spoke into a microphone concealed in his mask. "What do you see, Tick Tock?"

Team leader Tick Tock, Mickey Valient to the rest of the world, coordinated the car chase with the police. "It's our lucky day, boys. They're herding him right toward us."

In the growing winter darkness, the men stood nearly invisible in their midnight blue outfits, masks covering the upper half of their faces. When they spoke, their voices came out with a metallic distortion courtesy of Tick Tock's voice-disguising device.

Adrenaline rushed through his system as X waited on the ground. He missed being out with the guys. Had it only been two weeks? The rushed wedding and honeymoon had been exhilarating, but he was glad to be home and back at the work he loved.

Standing half-hidden in the alley, X grinned at his other friend and partner in crime-fighting. "Ready to play, big guy?"

Powerhouse, otherwise known as Bull Kincaid, smiled back, his pale skin and white teeth a sharp contrast against the dark mask. At least six and a half feet tall and built like a linebacker, Powerhouse usually played the "immovable object" against the unstoppable forces they came up against. He cracked his knuckles, then his neck. "Bring it," he said.

Police sirens wailed in the night, getting louder.

"How close?" X asked Tick Tock.

"Just turned down the alley," Tick Tock replied. "Get ready."

Powerhouse peeked around the fence that separated the alley from the parking lot where they waited. Gauging the distance to the approaching Toyota, he stepped back and moved behind an overflowing metal garbage bin. He placed his hands and one shoulder against it, waiting, shifting his weight from one foot to the other in anticipation.

X waited behind him, anxious for the fracas to begin. Sometimes he got to be the front man, but tonight they needed Powerhouse's muscle to end the chase. X tossed a short steel pipe from one hand to the other, feeling the rush of energy flow through his body. The gloves he wore were palm-less rather than fingerless. They protected him from leaving fingerprints, but allowed his skin to absorb the strength of the metal. He had been working on plans for flexible titanium-lined gloves before he met Tori, but the craziness of falling in love and getting married over the last two months had disrupted a lot of things. The gloves fell to the bottom of his to do list. Tonight he'd have to make do with the pipe.

X squeezed his right palm around the steel. Hot energy tightened his skin all over his body. The rush felt good. He put his new bride out of his mind and focused on the job at hand.

"Ready, set..." Tick Tock's voice came through their earpieces.

X shifted onto the balls of his feet in anticipation.

"Now!"

Powerhouse shoved the garbage bin into the alley. The squeal of brakes, the crash of metal on metal as the car hit the heavy steel container full-on. Powerhouse jumped behind the garbage bin and locked his elbows. He kept the car from skidding toward the surrounding buildings by digging his heels into the snow-covered asphalt. X watched the pavement buckle behind his friend's feet.

The car stopped with a final screech of damaged metal. X watched the doors for exiting passengers. His turn at bat.

The garbage bin began to roll toward the opposite building. Powerhouse pushed it to a flatter area. Less paperwork if there wasn't any damage to surrounding private property. X didn't like to waste time with paper when there were always more people to

protect, more criminals to catch.

"Driver side," came Tick Tock's voice in their ears.

The driver side door flew open and X took his position. A young man stumbled out — maybe old enough to vote, not old enough to drink, but dumb enough to run. He looked over his shoulder toward the approaching police car, his feet already double-timing in the opposite direction.

Right into the path of Superhero X.

Wham!

The young man slammed into him and fell.

X grinned down, tapping the pipe against his thigh. He had only an inkling of what it felt like for someone to run into him. His brothers said it was like running into a steel wall. X put his palm out and raised his fingers twice. The universal sign for "come and get it."

The driver gaped up at him from the pavement. One hand held his head. Must've cracked it on X's chest.

"He's not a mouse, X. Hold him for the officers." Tick Tock sounded either exasperated or amused. X couldn't tell through the voice-disguiser. "Powerhouse, another one on the passenger side."

X shook his head slightly. There was no challenge in it when things went according to plan. He reached down to grab the driver. Not quick enough.

The man rolled away. Standing, he now held a 9mm pistol. Jogging backwards with the gun aimed at X, he ducked between two buildings.

X muttered under his breath. Careful what you wish for. More squealing brakes signaled the arrival of the police. X gave chase. A cop pounded a few yards behind him.

"He's got a gun," X yelled over his shoulder.

More sirens sounded from the front of the building. Police shouted to each other. X struggled to hear Tick Tock in his earpiece.

"Say again?" he shouted as he ran.

"Turn right. Bushes in front."

The buildings gave way to the parking lot and X turned right.

Three more police officers came running from their cars at the front of the building. X paused, searching the snow for footprints. He saw movement, halogen security lights reflected a flash of red fabric. He bounded into the bushes just as the driver jumped up with his gun.

X pulled up short. A shootout was not the kind of excitement he was looking for. Too many ways for it to end badly. Putting out his hand in a conciliatory gesture, he turned his body to shield the police officers behind him. Slow movements and quiet words would win the day. "Now just—"

"Drop your weapon!" a cop behind him shouted.

The cop moved into X's peripheral vision on the left. Idiot. Didn't he know X was here to protect him? He was supposed to stay back. If the driver started shooting now, he could hit any of them.

The young man flinched at the cop's shout and raised his gun. To his left, X saw all the officers bring up their guns, everyone shouting at the guy to drop his weapon. X groaned. So much for slow movements and quiet words. The situation had spiraled out of control. Which left only one option.

Before anyone could start shooting, X leapt at the guy, holding tightly to the steel pipe. In a flash, an image of Tori appeared in his mind, a picture of his lovely little wife with a gun pointed at her. Another flash, and Tori was advancing on the gunman.

Protect her.

The same imperative voice that shouted in his mind when he first met Tori was stronger than ever. Along with the vision, it shook him, and X realized as he launched himself at the gun-wielding drug dealer that his timing was a half-second too late.

Bang! The gun went off.

TORI pulled her fisted hands from her coat pockets, looking

around, trying to decide what to do. *Please help me, God.* Her eyes darted to Eddie behind the counter. He saw the quiet man moving toward the gunman, too. Eddie opened the cash register and started counting the bills out loud.

"Twenty, forty, sixty—"

"Just put it in the bag, man!" the kid shouted.

Eddie shot him an angry look. "I have to tell my dad how much got stolen for the insurance paperwork, you idiot! Eighty, one hundred..." Eddie kept counting, picking up the tens and then the fives.

Tori felt her lips twitch in a tiny smile. Brilliant! The kid was so focused on the money, he didn't see the other guy sneaking up behind him. Tori tensed, praying this would work.

Crash!

Behind her, near the women, a glass jar fell and broke. The young woman screamed.

The gunman swung around. "Everybody freeze!"

More screams tore the air. Tori ducked as the kid waved the gun. The idiot looked like he was in a gangster movie. He probably didn't even know how to use the thing.

The gunman turned back to the cashier. "Give me the money and no one gets hurt!"

Eddie stopped counting and started putting the money into a paper bag. Tori thought he nodded to the other man, only four or five feet away now and gliding forward soundlessly.

When Eddie started to put all the change into the bag, the gunman interrupted him. "Forget the change! I don't want no change! What, you never been held up before? Get me the money from the safe, asshole, and I'm gone, and you live."

Eddie shook his head. "I-I can't — the safe—"

"Give him the money!" one of the women screamed.

The kid cocked his gun (okay, maybe he did know how to use it), looking back and forth between the customers and the cashier. As Tori watched from the cover of the candy aisle, the man behind the robber darted with amazing stealth first one way then the other,

always keeping out of the gunman's line of sight. How did he do that? He was over there, and then he was there, and then—

The robber didn't see it coming — the other man closed the distance, thrusting the kid's gun arm into the air, and shoving him into the counter. Eddie reached for the customary convenience store baseball bat, but he wasn't fast enough. The robber twisted under the other guy. The two men tussled. The women screamed. Eddie ducked, and—

A shot rang out!

Tori flinched and ducked again. Could she do something to help? But what? She pressed a fist into her stomach, trying to keep the roiling fear down so she could think. The hot feeling in her stomach grew as she struggled between self-preservation and the overwhelming urge to help keep everyone safe.

The robber jumped away as the other man fell to the floor.

Another crash of glass. The gunman whirled again. He pointed the gun at the man with the crying baby.

Not the baby! Not if she could stop him. Tori grabbed handfuls of yellow M&M'S packages and started throwing them at the gunman. "Don't shoot!" Tori screamed at him, hot anger bursting out. "Stop it! Put that gun down!"

The kid ducked her shots, candy hitting him in the face and shoulder, unable to keep the gun aimed any more. Tori marched toward him, too pissed off to think. Out of ammunition, she pointed her finger at him like a kindergarten teacher. *"Put it down now, mister!"*

The kid looked at her like she was crazy. Then with little hesitation, he put the gun on the counter.

A split second later, Eddie had the baseball bat against the robber's throat. As the guy clawed for air, the front door burst open and police officers crashed in, flowing through the room like a dam had burst.

Tori jumped out of their way, her hand pressed to her queasy stomach. Police threw the robber to the ground and cuffed him. One officer checked the man who had been shot while another

asked Eddie if he was okay. Tori noticed Eddie's bleeding head. When had that happened? The police waved in EMTs who worked on the guy with the bullet wound.

The hero of the day. Tori hoped he was okay. That was amazing the way he just — just stepped in and saved everyone. The guy was a real hero. And so was Eddie.

"Are you all right, ma'am?" Tori felt a policeman shake her shoulder.

"The guy that was shot…" she said, still watching the EMTs. She couldn't see the man himself. *God, please let him be okay.* She tried to focus on breathing, in and out, don't look at the blood.

"They're taking care of him. I'm sure he'll be fine. Are you hurt?"

"No, I — no." Tori tried to swallow but her mouth was bone dry. She noticed her hand hurt and looked down. Her fist had wrapped her purse strap in a death grip. She looked up at the policeman. "I thought he was going to shoot the baby." There was no way she could ever, *ever* let someone hurt a child.

The policeman smiled and said, "The baby is fine. See?"

Tori followed his pointing finger to see the man rocking his little girl, talking to another officer. They both looked fine. Then the man looked at Tori and pointed at her as he spoke.

It only took Tori a moment to realize why. She looked down at the floor littered with peanut M&M'S — yellow, green, blue, red, brown.

The policeman laughed. "I've never seen anyone take down a gunman in quite that way before."

"I'm sorry." Tori didn't know what to say. What had she been thinking? She never would have interfered like this a few months ago. The policeman questioned her about what had just happened, but Tori's mind darted around like a chickadee. Since she'd stopped seeing her psychiatrist and stopped taking her medications, she felt better than ever. Freer and more alive. But maybe she shouldn't allow herself to be quite so free. Walking up to a man with a gun!

The meds kept her from any kind of spontaneous action or

uncontrolled emotional response. Maybe that was better than, than...whatever just happened.

"Are you okay?" The policeman looked at her closely.

Tori wasn't sure of the correct response. She was alive — thank God — and she was going to see Joe again, and day eleven of married life. But...she wasn't exactly feeling well. Her stomach was calming down, but she felt herself beginning to shake from the inside out.

"Let's sit you down for a minute, shall we?" The policeman took her arm and escorted her outside toward his car.

The bitter cold night air helped clear her head. As they walked past the stretcher where the wounded man lay, Tori paused. Had everyone thanked him? He certainly deserved their gratitude. She bent down. But she didn't know what to say. What words were enough?

"You're very brave," she murmured, touching his uninjured shoulder briefly. "Thank you so much."

He glared back at her. "What? Your suit at the cleaners?" he whispered fiercely, "Or is this your day off?"

Tori pulled back a little. "What?" Why was he attacking her?

"I'd think a guy with a gun would be enough that you could use your powers before someone gets shot," he spat at her. "But no, had to be the hero, huh? Had to wait till you were the only superhero who could save the day. That's why I work alone. Superheroes like you are just super*egos*. You don't care about anything but your media image!"

The EMT moved Tori out of the way. She heard the man moan as they hustled him into the ambulance.

What was he talking about? When she called out to the gunman she was just...worried, scared. That's all. It was probably a stupid thing to do, but it distracted him enough so that Eddie could grab him.

The policeman put his arm around Tori as she swayed on her feet. He tucked her into the back seat of his police car. "Why don't you put your head down?" he suggested.

Tori shook her head. She just needed to get her bearings. The car was warm, and she closed her eyes, leaning back into the seat. She let her mind wander as she tried to relax. She tried not to think about what kinds of people had been sitting in the back of this police car lately. Could lice survive the winter? Ugh, best not to think about it.

Her thoughts returned to the conversation with the man who'd been shot. It hit her then — was he saying he was a superhero? Tori's eyes flew open and she turned in time to see the ambulance pull away. She'd met a superhero?

She flopped back against the seat. No. Impossible! Her parents had always insisted the "superhero" stories in the news were publicity stunts. Crime was on the rise and the city government would say anything to look like they had it under control.

She'd heard her mother's voice saying a hundred times over the years, "There's no such thing as superheroes. A few freaks out there who want to be more than they are, but no one has any kind of supernatural power."

Tori accepted this version of the world. It made sense. It was logical, orderly. To believe that people might have supernatural abilities opened the door to possibilities Tori didn't want to consider. She and her sister Lexie had enough freak factor with the strange things that sometimes happened around them.

This guy accusing her of being a superhero did seem a little freaky, that's true. Of course, he'd been shot, lost blood, was probably out of his mind with pain. But that other guy…

Tori's mind drifted back for a moment to Halloween. Some kid had grabbed her purse and taken off. Tori chased him, but she tripped and fell. Moments later a man dressed as Zorro appeared, gorgeous and thrilling. He helped her get her purse back, and picked her up like she weighed no more than a doll. Then he kissed her like—

Tori shook her head and opened her eyes. Sure it was a great kiss, but she never saw him again. She met Joe a couple days later, fell madly in love with him, and married him on Christmas Eve.

She straightened her shoulders. She had no intention of thinking about another man now that she was married. But she wondered if her parents were wrong. Maybe superheroes did exist. If so, they weren't all freaks. Not Zorro anyway.

Still, why would this possible "superhero" accuse *her* of being a superhero? Maybe in the pain of getting shot, he…got confused. In her mind's eye, Tori saw the look on the robber's face as he put the gun down. There was something about it, something familiar. Her mind tripped and twisted with roiling emotions and panic-infused imagination. She needed to stop this crazy thinking.

But her brain wouldn't stop working on it. Now she remembered. Last night when she and Joe had stopped over at her sister Lexie's and little Ben wouldn't go to bed, she'd used her Aunt Tori voice and forcefully insisted he go to bed. He'd looked at her with that same funny look on his face. Then he did. The barely-three-year-old turned and went to his room without another word.

And a few months ago. When Lexie told her that it wasn't just that Tori could convince people of things, but that she could force people to *do* things. And Lexie had only said that because — oh my gosh, that's right — Tori had *insisted* that Lexie tell her what she was thinking.

Tori felt her breath coming quicker but she couldn't catch it, she couldn't breathe. She kept trying to breathe, but the air just kept going in and out of her mouth without hitting her lungs and she couldn't get a breath and—

The door opened and the policeman said something but Tori couldn't catch his words and then he was pushing her head onto her knees and still talking and she thought she heard, "That's it. Breathe."

Tori gulped in air, then tried to slow down and get the blood to stop pounding in her head. It's not possible. It simply wasn't possible to live for twenty-seven years and not know…not make the connection.

She'd test it. Then she'd know. It wouldn't work, and then she'd know her mother was right. There was no such thing as superheroes.

No such thing as super powers.

Tori looked up at the cop. "I need some M&M'S. I went in for M&M'S and I need them, please." She knew she was jabbering, but she had to know. "Please get me some."

"Just take a deep breath and—"

She glared into his eyes, hoping and terrified and feeling very, very alone. Her gut burned with heat. *"I need M&M'S! Please!"*

The cop stopped in the middle of his sentence. He looked at her for a moment, then stood up and turned back toward the store. When he came back with every kind of M&M'S flavor the store sold, Tori fainted.

A Note From Kitty

I hope you enjoyed reading *A Very Merry Superhero Wedding* as much as I enjoyed writing it! I never intended to write this story when I started the Adventures of Lewis and Clarke series, but the idea is fascinating to me. How can two people meet and immediately know that they want to spend the rest of their lives together — and then do it successfully?

If you enjoyed this book, check out the short story prequel, "Superhero in Disguise," the story of how Tori and Joe met on Halloween, and *Unexpected Superhero*, book one in the Adventures of Lewis and Clarke series, where Tori finds out why she's different.

I love connecting with my readers, so please sign up for my newsletter on my web site and say hi on social media!

Web site: http://kittybucholtz.com
Facebook: www.facebook.com/kittybucholtzauthor
Twitter: @KittyBucholtz

And if you really want to make my day, I'd love for you to post your thoughts about the book in a review. Thanks so much!

If you haven't read it yet and you like romantic comedies with a chick-lit style of writing, check out my first book, *Little Miss Lovesick*.

About the Author

Kitty Bucholtz grew up forty miles east of Traverse City, Michigan — a town that is a smaller but surprisingly similar version of Double Bay, Michigan, the setting of this book. She went to college in Traverse City, met and married the love of her life, and waved goodbye to everything she knew when she and her husband John struck out for parts unknown.

Their adventures included going back to school, changing careers, and traveling Down Under. They spent three years in Sydney, Australia, where Kitty earned her M.A. in Creative Writing from University of Technology, Sydney, while John made a penguin named Mumble dance. Kitty now writes wherever John is working on a film.

Only God knows where they'll wind up next — but they're pretty sure it will be another cool chapter in their adventure!

Book Clubs!

If you would like to read *A Very Merry Superhero Wedding* with your book club, Kitty has a gift to send you and your club members! You can also plan a video call with Kitty and your club.

For details, email your name, email address, phone number (optional), and city/time zone to kitty@kittybucholtz.com.

Made in the USA
Charleston, SC
17 March 2015